Wifey's Next HUSTLE

KS Publications
www. kikiswinson. net

DON'T MISS OUT ON THESE OTHER TITLES:

How It All Began

After the near-death situation I had put myself in and the lost of a person I loved dearly, I left my hometown for good, gave up being *Wifey,* and ventured into selling high-end cars such as Ashton Martins, Rolls Royce's and Lamborghinis at a luxury car dealership in South Beach, Florida. My clients consisted of wealthy cats such as Hedge Fund Investors and dope boys. I get more dope boys in my office than corporate executives, but who's counting. Today my favorite client by the name of Kendrick Miles stopped by to inquire about the new Rolls Royce Phantom we brought in the night before. Kendrick was a very handsome guy. In fact, he put me in the mind of Kevin Hart but with more height. He always smelled good when he was in my company, so today was no different. "Hi there beautiful," he said when he walked across the threshold of my office. This was Kendrick's typical behavior. He always greeted me by calling me beautiful. He was a charmer at heart. I was definitely one of his favorite people unless I couldn't give him a good price on a car, and then he'd call me Kira.

His smile lit up my entire office. He had the most beautiful set of teeth I'd ever seen. I often wondered how he kept them so white. His clothing game was on point too. He swore by Tom Ford and I see why.

I stood up from my chair and gave him a warm embrace. The touch of his physique was magical. My panties stayed wet while I was around him. "What cha' got for me today?" he asked.

I sat back down and started clicking away at my computer keys. "Of course, I've got something for you. We just got a few new cars in yesterday and I'm sure you're gonna love every one of them." I smiled, taking my attention off of the computer screen for a second.

"Well, let's get down to business." He said eagerly.

I stood back up from my chair and escorted Kendrick and his right hand man to the showroom floor. "Take a look at this gorgeous, white Rolls-Royce Phantom Drop-head Coupe." I introduced as we entered into the private quarters of the dealership. This room was designed specifically for VIP clients. The recess lights placed in the ceiling of this room gave the cars perfect lighting.

"What's the price tag on this?" he wondered aloud as he walked around the vehicle checking out all the detail.

"Trust me, it's within your price range." I uttered softly as I followed him around the car. "Get inside

and let's see how good you look behind the wheel."
I suggested as I opened the driver side door.

Kendrick took a seat behind the wheel of the car
and started inspecting the interior along with the features built into the dashboard. "How fast is it?" He
asked.

"Because this model has a V-12 engine it goes
from zero to 60mph in less than six seconds."

"What is the mileage per gallon?"

"The city is eleven and the highway is eighteen."

"How much horsepower are we talking?" his
questions continued as he adjusted the rearview mirror.

"Four hundred and fifty-three."

"Sounds enticing." He commented as he looked
over his shoulders into the backseat.

"I thought you'd say that." I commented, giving
him the biggest smile I could muster up. Kendrick
was a man of many words and he had the pocketful
of money to back it up.

"So, what am I looking at in terms of the price?
And if I decide to buy it, when can I have it delivered
to me?"

"Well if you wire me four and three quarters, I
can have it delivered to you tomorrow." I spoke confidently.

Kendrick started moving the steering wheel.
"Four and three quarters, huh?" he said aloud. He
was definitely in thought mode.

"Yes. And with all the features this vehicle has, you're getting a damn good price." I interjected. I had to convince him that this half a million-dollar price tag was a steal. Not only would I be getting a huge commission, I could potentially become one of the district managers around here. The field of car selling was male dominated, so I had to prove myself worthy in this place.

"I'll tell you what," he started off saying. "I will have my bank wire you the money right now if you'll agree to help me with a problem I have."

Shocked by his odd request, I wanted to know what kind of problem he had. And I also wanted to know how he thought I'd be able to help him. "What's going on?" I asked him.

He stepped out of the car and closed the driver side door. "Can we go back to your office so we can talk in private?"

"Yes, sure. Of course," I replied and then I escorted he and his bodyguard back to my office. Kendrick's bodyguard stood by the door while Kendrick and I took a seat.

Before he told me about his dilemma, he went into a spiel about how long he's known me and how he has sent me a lot of business whether it was with him or other guys he referred. To add icing to the cake, he even mentioned how he's sent me on lavish vacations around the world. Kendrick was pouring the guilt factor on really thick and I knew that if I hadn't stopped him, he would've kept talking. "What's on your mind?" I broke the ice.

"You said your father is a retired Circuit Court judge, right?"

I hesitated before I answered his question. I wanted to know where he was going with this but I was afraid to ask. "Yes," I finally said.

"Well, here's the thing," he began to say, "there's a judge in the Circuit Court by the name of Judge Mahoney that just retired a few days ago......"

"Yeah I know him. My father used to invite he and his wife over for parties and barbecues before my mother passed away." I blurted out.

"That's perfect. So, what I need you to do is help me find out where this judge lives because we have some unfinished business with him." Kendrick said.

Alarmed by the urgency of him wanting to find Judge Mahoney, I began to feel a little uneasy. "You aren't trying to kill him are you?" I asked, giving him a half smile. I couldn't let him see how nervous I had become. It didn't work.

"Look Kira, everything is cool. Nobody is getting hurt. I just need to talk to him. And after that, I'm going on about my way."

"Can you tell me what he did?" I probed. I needed some assurance that Mr. Mahoney wasn't going to get hurt like Kendrick had just promised.

"I'd rather not get into that. But I will say that everything will be alright after I get a chance to speak with him."

I hesitated to speak. I honestly didn't know what to say in response to Kendrick's plea for my help.

"So, when can you make this happen?" Kendrick wanted to know.

"Give me a couple of days. I need to figure out how to ask my dad about him without bringing any unnecessary attention to it.

"Well, do what you got to do to make it happen. And when you get me what I need, hit me up at this number." He said as he stood up to his feet and then handed me a phone number written on a plain white looking business card.

"What about the car?" I asked after I cuffed the card in my hand.

"Don't worry about that. I'll have the money wired over to you in the next thirty minutes, so get my paperwork ready and make sure I get my car by noon tomorrow."

"Will do," I replied as I watched Kendrick and his flunky walk out of my office.

Where There's Dick
– There's Pussy

After having a long day I retreated to my apartment in the sky. Collins Avenue was the place to be in Miami, especially if you loved the water. The Atlantic Ocean was literally outside my apartment. The balcony located in the living room of my apartment gave me the perfect view. I couldn't ask for more.

While I was entering into apartment, my man Dylan greeted me. He stood in the foyer with a chilled glass of red wine in his hand and the biggest smiled he could muster up. His smile was infectious so I had to smile back at him. "I hope that's for me." I commented as I stepped out of my heels and dropped my handbag and car keys onto the table in the foyer.

"Of course it is," he replied as he handed me the glass.

I took a sip of the wine and allowed the smoothness of the alcohol to go down my throat slowly. "Ummm, this is good."

"Did you expect anything different?"

Instead of answering his question, I gave him a wet kiss. I sucked on his bottom lip and started massaging his dick with my other hand. It didn't take long for him to get an erection. "Ready to slide all of this dick in my pussy?" I whispered to him after I released him from my kiss. I looked into his eyes and waited for him to answer me.

"You know I am," he said, his voice sounded sexy, but masculine.

I put the glass of wine to my mouth and downed the rest of it. After the glass was empty I sat it down on the table next to my car keys. "Wanna fuck me from the back?" I asked him.

"Let's do it," he replied and started unzipping his pants.

I turned around to face the table and then I placed both of my hands on the edge of it. I stuck out my butt and then I looked over my shoulder. "Come and get it." I instructed him. Without hesitation, he pulled up my pencil skirt, pulled my G-string to the side and buried himself deep inside of me. The impact of his massive dick plowed inside of me making me feel a multitude of feelings. "Mmmmm, this feels so good," I moaned. My pussy was wet as hell. In fact, he made my pussy as creamy as ever.

"Yes, this shit feels good as hell. Mmmm, mmm," he said as he held onto my hips and gyrated against me. The electric shocks I felt while he pushed himself in and out of me went straight to my heart. I was really in love with his man. "Baby, please don't let me go," I begged, in an exotic way.

"I won't." he promised as he continued to make love to me.

"Ahhh," I screamed out as he pound me harder and harder. I felt my ass jiggling with every move he made. "Oh God! Oh God! Oh God!" I hollered. My moans made him excited more than ever now.

"C'mon . . . give it to me," I instructed him. He was moving at a steady pace but I knew it was about to change.

"Owww! Yeah fuck me baby! Fuck me harder." I screamed. By this time he was fucking me so hard, my head started jerking back and forth.

"Oh shit, girl, your pussy is out of this fucking world," Dylan growled.

I started to feel myself about to cum because the shaft of his dick was pressing on my g-spot. "I'm coming!" I called out. The pressure in my vagina was about to explode. Busting a nut was only ten seconds away and I was ready. "Baby, I'm about to cum." I said softly, but in a seductive way.

"Cum on this dick." He instructed as he continued to grind his dick inside of me. The feeling of his stiff manhood sent chills all through my body. He knew exactly how to hold my hips while he gave me every inch of his dick. With each stroke came a deeper feeling of love from him. He was a master of this. It felt like he was giving me his all. Sparks were flying. "Agggghhhh!" Dylan bucked and screamed. He was coming as well. I could feel every ounce of his cum filter inside of me.

"Owwww, baby you make my pussy feel so good! I gasped while I was bucking back and forth.

After Dylan finished emptying all of his juices in me, his dick went limp and that's when he backed away from me. He looked exhausted. "It felt like a workout, huh?" I joked.

"Nah, I'm good. You know I aim to please." He smiled and turned to leave. I watched him walk into the bathroom only a few feet away from me.

I pushed my skirt down, grabbed my empty wine glass and headed into the kitchen. Immediately after I placed the glass in the sink I headed to my bedroom so I could freshen up. It took me less than fifteen minutes to shower and change into a Vicky t-shirt and a pair of jean shorts. I called my attire, *walk around the house* attire.

"Looking good!" Dylan commented after he entered into the bedroom and sat down on the edge of the bed. He liked watching me prance around. He often told me how obsessed he was with my body. I never told him this, but all my past men were obsessed with my body too, even though they cheated on me numerous times.

"Don't come in here harassing me." I joked while I stood in the mirror combing my hair up into a ponytail.

"How was work today?"

"It was great. Got one of my VIP customers to purchase the 2014 Rolls Royce Coupe. And it's gonna be delivered to him tomorrow."

"Do I know 'em?" Dylan asked me. I knew where this conversation was going. Dylan had this thing about my male customers. He knew how beautiful I was and he knew men wanted me bad. I've always assured him that he had nothing to worry about. But Dylan was bullheaded so he wasn't trying to hear me.

"Yes, you know him."

"Who is it?"

"Kendrick."

"Wait a minute, wasn't he just in your office a month ago copping that red Ferrari?"

"Yes he was."

"So, he's a VIP customer because he copped a Rolls Royce?" Dylan questioned me.

I turned around from the mirror so I could face him. I even gave him the spoiled little brat face. "Baby, please let's not fight tonight. We just had some great sex so I want the night to end on a nice note."

"Look, I don't trust that nigga. He's bad news. My partner and I didn't stop doing business with him because he talked badly about us in the streets. He damaged a good relationship that we had with our South American connection. We had been doing business with the Rodriquez family for years. So when we cut off ties with them it set us back tremendously."

"Baby, I understand where you stand with Kendrick, which is why it's strictly business. And once he leaves my office, that's where the buck stops."

"You know I told you that you don't have to work. I've got more money than we can count. We're straight for life." Dylan said. He acted like he was shouting out to the world.

"I know baby. I know." I replied as I began to walk towards him.

As soon as I got within arms reach, he pulled me into a bear hug and I looked directly into his eyes. "I love you so much." I said softly.

"Well then, let me take care of you." He interjected.

"Look at this apartment, you're already taking care of me."

"That's not what I'm talking about. I don't want you to lift a finger. I wanna marry you and have a couple of kids, so I can have a real family." He announced.

I was shocked beyond belief. I mean, I knew he wanted to marry me but to settle down and bring children in this world added some seriousness to the equation, especially after all the drama I had with the lovers in my past.

"Dylan listen, I want everything you want, but can you give me some time?" I said and then I kissed him on his lips.

"Okay," he replied.

"Good, now let's go into the kitchen and find something to eat." I suggested and then I grabbed his hand and lead him down the hallway. While we were in the kitchen, we made small talk about going on a vacation. It was my idea to go to Hawaii. He wanted to go on a cruise to Europe. I wasn't a Europe vacationer. I wanted to feel a lot of sand between my toes and lay out on the beach. So, I figured that either Dylan was going to let me have my way or he's going to have to pay me another way, by taking me on a serious shopping spree. I knew he'd do it with no problem. He was a sweetheart when he wanted to be. Dylan was a grown man for real. He represented cats from the south. He had that southern hospitality and I loved that about him.

Was I Now a Private Eye?

The very next morning I stopped by my father's house before I headed to work. I figured this would be a good time to get the ball rolling and hopefully get the information Kendrick needed to find Judge Mahoney. And even though Dylan had forbidden me from doing anything for Kendrick outside of the office, I went against his wishes because I really didn't have a choice. Kendrick was a master manipulator and he always got what he wanted, no matter the cost. Besides that, Kendrick has done a lot for me even before Dylan came into my life so that was another reason why I went against him. I figured that this little favor wouldn't take up too much of my time, and after I give Kendrick the information he needs, it will all be over. My debt would be paid in full.

My dad was sitting on the living room sofa, legs propped on the coffee table and heavily engrossed in the business section of a new issue of Forbes magazine. "Hey daddy. How has your morning been so far?" I greeted him immediately after I entered into the room.

He laid the magazine down on his lap and gave me the biggest smile ever. I leaned down towards him and kissed him on his cheek. And after I sat down on the sofa next to him, I opened up a floodgate of questions. "So, what's going on with you?" I said, trying to chip away the ice gradually.

"What you see is what you get." He smiled.

I looked at my father and couldn't deny how handsome he was. He was the spitting image of the lead singer from Frankie Beverly and Maze. The salt and pepper hair mixed together in his beard made him look more distinguished than ever. "Daddy, you need to get you a woman." I said.

"And you need a husband. Because if I remember correctly you and your boyfriend have been living together for over a year and a half now and he's yet to pop the question." He replied sarcastically.

"Daddy, I didn't come over here to talk about my marital status with Dylan."

"Well, we need to. And where is he now anyway?"

"He was at the apartment when I left."

"You know I'm still in the dark about what it is that he does for a living."

"Daddy, I told you he and his family own several businesses together." I replied confidently.

"Yeah, yeah, yeah." My father commented and picked up his magazine. He wasn't buying anything I was selling. He was a very sharp man so it was hard to feed him bullshit, especially when it came to Dylan. My father has always had his suspicions about Dylan. No matter how much I harped on the fact that he owned several businesses with his partner Will, my father knew that there was more to the story. He'd write me out of his will if he knew Dylan was a bad boy in every sense of the word. But of course, he'd never find that out from me. My lips were sealed.

"I'm gonna go on one of those dating sites and find you a female companion." I said jokingly, shifting the focus away from Dylan.

"I don't need you to do that for me. I told you I am fine. Women require too much attention and I'm too old to learn the ways of another woman all over again. It takes too much energy."

"You know what daddy, I can't agree with you more." I sided with him. "So, what are you getting into later?" My questions kept coming. I had to lead up to the question of the day.

"Nothing much. I was thinking about going out to get me some ice cream. And that should be about it."

"Why don't you hang out with your friends that you used to work with?" I blurted out. I was warming up and treading very lightly with how I questioned my dad. He was a very smart man. He was also a retired judge so he's seen the most disheartening criminals Florida has to offer, so believe me he could see bullshit from far away.

"I get with my buddies from time to time for a few games of golf."

"But you don't get out enough daddy. I think you should call your friend Judge Mahoney. Maybe he can come by and keep you company. You know play a few games of chess." I replied.

"I've hung out with him a couple of times. I just haven't spoken with him since he hung up his robe a few days ago. But I'm sure he'll reach out to me for a couple of games of golf after he gets back from the keys."

"So, he's still in the area?"

"Of course he is. His wife has family here in Miami so she's not letting him move anywhere."

"Are they still living over there near Olympia Heights?" I asked my father. I've never known where Judge Mahoney and his wife lived but I figured if I threw out a name of one of Miami's gated communities, I would trick my father into telling me where they really resided.

"No, he lives on Largo Drive in the Coral Gables section of Miami."

"Oh it's beautiful over there." I commented.

"Yes. It's really nice. As a matter of fact, he bought himself a nice boat right before he retired. He said that he and I are going to do some fishing as soon as he ties up a few loose ends."

I thought for a moment after hearing my father say that Judge Mahoney just bought himself a boat and that they're going on a fishing trip after he tied up some loose ends. This sounded fishy to me. What loose ends was Judge Mahoney talking about? Did those loose ends have something to do with Kendrick? Sooner than later the truth will surface.

Paying My Debt

I got Kendrick on the line immediately after I left my father's house. One of his boys answered the cell phone number he gave me before he left my office yesterday. "Can I speak with Kendrick?" I asked.

"Hold on," the guy said. I heard a little rambling from the other end and then I heard Kendrick say hello.

"Hey Kendrick, I got that information you wanted." I told him.

"Where are you?"

"I'm in my car and on my way to work." I replied.

"Give me thirty minutes and I'll meet you at your office." He said and then I heard a click.

"Hello," I said but Kendrick did not answer. So, I took my cell phone away from my ear and looked at the screen and realized that he disconnected out call. It was so abrupt. I mean, damn! What happened to proper phone etiquette? It was apparent that this guy didn't have any. Or he was one of those guys that didn't like talking over the phone. I've been with enough niggas to know that the phone makes cats paranoid, especially when you lived that life.

The dealership's district manager Jason Wheeler called me into his office as soon as I walked into the dealership. Jason was a middle-aged, Jewish guy from New York. He had a wife and a couple of kids but he was always at work. Talk about dedication. "Kira, I asked you to come to my office to personally congratulate you on your sales this month. You've brought in over $10,000,000 and we're only half way through the month."

I smiled. "Really," I said in a humbling manner. I had already known where my sales were. I was the only chick working at this dealership so I had something to prove. And it didn't hurt that I knew a lot of drug dealers. I was on cloud nine.

"Keep it up and you're gonna be promoted to the manager's position in no time."

"Thank you." I said and then I slid out of his office. I wasn't about to let Jason's ass talk me too death. I didn't want a damn manager's position. I was fine where I was. Commission sounds a lot better than long hours. From what I've seen, Jason spends more time here than at home. There's no way Dylan is going to allow me to be at work that much. It would ever happen.

On my way to my office, I saw one of my old customers named Phillip Newsome. He was the owner of Club Lux, one of the hottest nightclubs in Miami. He was a fucking ladies man. I sold him a Lamborghini about eight months ago and now he's back for a new toy. What's funny about this scene was that his bitch ass wasn't copping his next car through me. I guess he's still bitter about the fact that I refused to go out on a date with him and give him some pussy. That's not my M.O. And besides, I've got a man at home who's got plenty of money. He reminds me constantly that I don't need this job so maybe I need to let Phillip talk to Dylan or a minute for two. Dylan would sure set the record straight.

When I finally got to my office I started working on some of the paperwork I had sitting on the corner of my desk. With the mindset that I was going to finish it all, Kendrick and that same guy stopped by the dealership like he said he would. I was on a call with another VIP customer when he walked into my office. "Mrs. Juarez, your car will be ready later this evening. So I will call you as soon as I get word." I said and then I hung up the phone.

Kendrick took a seat in the chair placed in front of my desk while this bodyguard stood by the door. "Can you close the door please?" I asked the guy.

"Yeah, close the door." Kendrick instructed him.

After the guy closed the door Kendrick went straight into question mode. "So, what do you have for me?" he asked.

"Well, after talking to my father I found out that Judge Mahoney resides on Largo Drive in Coral Gables and he just bought a nice boat for his retirement gift."

"Oh really?" Kendrick replied as he peeled away a slip of sticky paper from the colorful note pad and a pen from my deck. I watched him write down the street address and he seemed very annoyed.

"Is everything okay?" I asked, even though I knew that it wasn't.

Kendrick tossed the pen on my desk and stuffed the sticky note into his inside jacket pocket. "Have you gotten the money my people wired to you yet?" he asked, changing the subject.

"Yes, the accounting office received it yesterday so they're finishing your paperwork as we speak."

"Sounds good." He said and then he stood up from his seat. "Nice doing business with you."

But before he could leave my office, Dylan popped out of nowhere, toting a crystal vase with over two dozen pink roses. Kendrick saw the expression on my face and looked in the direction I was looking. And when he realized that I was looking at Dylan he smiled and said, "Looks like you got a special delivery." I knew Kendrick was being an asshole because of the beef he and Dylan had but I wasn't feeding into it. I instructed Kendrick's bodyguard to step aside so Dylan could get into my office.

After Kendrick's henchman moved out of Dylan's way, Dylan walked into my office and placed the vase on my desk. "Hi baby," I said in a cheerful manner. I tried to make this sudden meeting less awkward as possible. But it didn't work. Kendrick had to be the one to ruffle Dylan's feathers.

"So, they got you down at the flower shop on 25th Street now, huh?"

"I own it. Right along with half of all the businesses in Miami." Dylan came back at him.

"Lighten up man, I was only trying to put a smile on your face." Kendrick continued as he made his way out of my office. His bodyguard stood by the door until Kendrick got completely in the hallway.

"Thanks for coming by." I spoke up while I watched him leave.

"Don't mention it." I heard him say while he was walking down the hallway to leave the dealership. The entire dealership was made up of mostly glass so I could see Kendrick as he and his bodyguard got into his car. Kendrick owned a fleet of cars, all bought from me of course. Today Kendrick's bodyguard was driving him around in his smoke grey Maserati. The Maserati was customized with bulletproof tinted windows, special front and rear lighting and tires. Kendrick's obsession for all the extra bells and whistles was very important to him, especially if and when he'd have a run-in with another street cat and bullets start ringing out. He'd have a good chance of leaving the scene unharmed. But if he continued to test cats out in the open like he had just done Dylan, things may not end in his favor.

After Kendrick left, Dylan was seething at the mouth. Whatever gesture he planned to make by bringing me those roses went straight out of the window. I asked him to sit down and he refused to do it. Instead, he hovered over my desk like he was about to interrogate me.

"Did you see that bullshit that just happened?" he spat. He knew not to raise his voice due to the fact that I was at work. So he grinded his teeth while the veins near his temple doubled in size.

I let out a long sigh. "Yes,"

"So, now do you see why I don't want you doing business with him? That nigga is cutthroat and he's a fucking rat!" he said.

"Look Dylan let's not get all bent out of shape. He's gone now so can we change the subject?" I pleaded. I wasn't in the mood to argue or debate with Dylan about how fucked up Kendrick was. Okay he was a fucking asshole. So be it. All I was interested in was making a big commission off of him. That was it.

"I want this to be the last time you deal with him. If he wants to buy another car, let one of these other guys around here take care of him." Dylan instructed me. It sounded more like he was trying to tell me what to do.

"You're kidding, right?" I asked him. I smiled hoping he was only pulling my leg.

"No I am not. I will not have a nigga disrespecting me in front of my woman and act like that shit is cool. Now do I make myself clear?" he roared. This time around I knew he meant business.

I was reluctant to give in but I said yes.

After Dylan went ham on me, he left my office. I didn't see or hear from him again until I got home later. I could tell he had calmed down after that blow up he had in my office earlier. I wanted to step to him about how he handled things with me after Kendrick left, but I left well enough alone. Dylan was a good man. And I knew he was only doing what he felt was necessary. End of story.

Fuck Whatcha' Heard

Because of the drama that unfolded yesterday with Kendrick and Dylan I decided to use one of my vacation days and spend the day with Dylan. He was very happy after he found out that I wasn't going into work today. "I've planned a whole day for us." He began to say while we were both dressed in our nightclothes, sitting at the kitchen table eating a bowl of oatmeal. "We're gonna go to the spa and get massages. Then we're gonna see a movie. And before the night is over, we're gonna go out and have a few drinks at our favorite spot."

"Sounds like we're going to have a busy day." I pointed out.

"Yes, we will. So, hurry up and finish eating so you can get dressed. I wanna be out of here within the next hour."

"I gotcha' baby. I will be ready." I assured him.

Like I had promised, I showered and was dressed within the timeframe Dylan gave me. So, we were out of our apartment and in his car in less than fifty-two minutes. Dylan was a stickler for time. I was the procrastinator but somehow we've managed to meet in the middle. Believe me, it took a lot of practice to get us there.

Our first stop was the Spa Bar. This Asian ran establishment was a very popular place for affluent people. Normally you'd have to make appointments months in advance but Dylan's family knew the owners well so we were able to secure a spot without any hassles. Ten seconds after we checked in, Dylan gets a phone call from his sister. "What's wrong Sonya?" I heard him say.

I couldn't hear what she was saying but from the looks of Dylan's facial expression, I knew something was not right. "Where is he now?" Dylan said.

Sonya said a few more words but they were all jumbled up.

"Okay, don't worry about it. I'll take care of it." He continued and then he disconnected her call.

"Is everything all right?" I asked.

"We're gonna have to reschedule our massages." He told me.

"Okay. I'm fine with that." I replied.

After we spoke with the receptionist and changed our appointment, Dylan and I hopped in his SUV and then he sped off towards the highway. He was quiet during the first couple of minutes of the drive but I stopped all of that. I wanted to know what was wrong and where were we going.

"I gotta stop by my mother's house. Sonya just told me that she thinks Bruce put his hands on my mama, because she saw a couple of bruises on her arms and her face."

"Where is Sonya now?"

"She said she just left mom's house to go to work."

"And where is your mother?

"Sonya said she's at the house by herself."

"So, where is Bruce?"

"She said he was gone when she got there."

"Well you know she's going to deny that he hit her." I commented.

"Not this time." Dylan said. He was serious.

"Well, would you prepare yourself just in case she does?" I told him. I was a woman and I knew what it felt like for a nigga to put his hands on me. I denied it until my face turned blue and I finally got tired of getting my head bashed in, then I walked away. It was as simple as that. I never told Dylan about my past discretions. And where I stood with it, he didn't need to know.

When we arrived at his mother's house whom I call Mrs. Daisy, we saw her late model E-Class Mercedes Benz sedan parked in the driveway. Before Dylan could park the car properly he jumped out of it and rushed towards the front door. He had a spare key to her house so he was in there in less than five seconds flat. I took my time to go inside the residence. I wanted Dylan to say whatever he needed to say to his mother before I walked into the house.

After waiting in the car for almost five minutes I walked into the house and found Dylan and Mrs. Daisy sitting at the kitchen table talking. I greeted her and asked her if I could use the bathroom. "Yeah baby, go ahead. You know where it is." She told me.

"Thank you," I said and turned around towards the bathroom and began to walk that way.

Inside the bathroom I could hear Dylan telling his mother that he's going to kill Bruce when he sees him. "I'm not gonna have a nigga walking around here putting his damn hands on you. I'd be less than a man if I did that." Dylan roared.

"But I told you that he didn't do this. I told you I fell when I was trying to change the light bulbs in the living room and fell down off the ladder." She tried to explain, but Dylan wasn't trying to hear that foolishness. Even I didn't believe that shit she was saying.

Dylan's mother was a fifty-five year old lady. Dylan's father was a gangster from back in the day and landed himself a life sentence in prison after orchestrating a massive hit on an entire family that tried to run him out of the drug business. Two months after Dylan's father went to prison to serve his life sentence he was killed by another inmate. Dylan knew the hit was put out on his father in retaliation from other members of that family so when

Dylan put out a hit of his own, that inmate was moved out of the prison. Some say he started co-operating with the Feds. Some say that he was killed. But no one really knew what happened.

I sat in the bathroom for a few more minutes. I even cut on the water a few times so Mrs. Daisy wouldn't feel embarrassed knowing that I could hear their little chat. "Look mama, I don't care what you say, I'm gonna have a talk with Bruce today and if he ain't saying what I wanna hear, I am going to hurt him really bad." I heard Dylan say.

"Honey, you are working yourself up for nothing. I told you I fell. That's it." Mrs. Daisy said, trying to convince Dylan but he wasn't buying it.

"Mama, I'm done with this conversation. So, tell Bruce I'm looking for him."

"You're wasting your time Dylan. I already told you what happened."

"No mama, what you're telling me is a lie. You don't deserve to be hit on like you're a freaking punching bag. That guy is a loser mama and you know it."

"He is not a loser Dylan. He is my husband. And you're gonna have to respect him."

"Mama, I'm not trying to hear that. Bruce is an alcoholic and he does not deserve to have you."

"You're entitled to having your own opinion. But Bruce is still my husband."

"Okay, well tell your husband to move you out of this house and buy you another one."

"For what? This is my house."

"Yeah, and my father is the one who bought it for you. Not that loser you got staying here."

"Dylan, I'm done with this conversation." I heard Mrs. Daisy say and then I heard a chair move across the floor. I knew then that their conversation was over.

To make things seem less awkward I came out of the bathroom. When I walked into the hallway Mrs. Daisy was walking straight towards me. I smiled at her. "I see you put some new wall paper in the bathroom."

"Yes, I did. You like it?" She smiled back.

"I love it." I told her.

She grabbed my hand and shook it. Then she patted me on my back. After I walked past her I looked back and saw a bruise on her face. It definitely looked like she was hit.

"Kira, come on let's go," Dylan called out.

"I'm coming." I replied.

We met at the front door and walked out the house together. "Mom, come and lock your door." Dylan yelled.

Mrs. Daisy didn't respond, but we knew she'd come and lock the door after we left.

"Why the fuck is she always taking up for that loser?" Dylan snapped. He hadn't driven off the block before he went into a rant.

"Because she's trying to protect him." I said.

"But why? He's a fucking unemployed alcoholic." Dylan barked. I knew that if he saw Bruce right now, he'd kill him.

"Your mother doesn't see it like that."

"If my father was still alive, he'd kill that nigaa for sure."

"And if your father was still alive, your mother wouldn't be with that guy."

Dylan didn't respond. He just shook his head back and forth like he was contemplating on doing something very sinister.

"Baby, whatever you're thinking, please stop it because you may regret it later." I pleaded.

"Fuck that clown! My father would disown me if he was still alive and he knew I let that nigga get away with hitting my mama. So, I've gotta get rid of him once and for all."

I wanted to make another plea for Bruce but I knew it would fall on death ears. I was beginning to learn that Dylan was just like my past men. The only difference was that he really loved and wanted to protect me. So, if I tried to intervene in this situation dealing with Bruce, he'd feel like I was going against the grain. In the end, I basically told him that whatever he did, he needed to be very careful and make sure he cleaned up his tracks.

Gotta' Stay On My Toes

I was standing in the lobby of the dealership when a couple walked through the front glass doors and approached me. The woman was a Hispanic, big booty chick who looked to be in her mid twenties. She was dressed in a beautiful, gold and white sundress that covered most of her legs. I had no idea who the designer was but when I saw the 4-inch, gold, metal, laser-cut butterfly sandals, I knew she was rocking a $1,100 pair of Sergio Rossi shoes. The white, $15,000 Hermes' Birken bag made her whole ensemble come together.

Her man was black. He looked to be in his early forties. In my eyes he was her sugar daddy. I thought his walk was nice. He was well groomed. He wore a dark blue Marc Jacobs polo shirt, a black pair of cargo shorts and a pair of black, Croc-embossed, Jimmy Choo sneakers.

When they got within arms reach he introduced them both to me while we shook hands. "Hi, my name is Brian and this is my lady Lizette. And we're here to check out a few cars for her." He said pointing to Lizette.

I looked at her from head to toe, sizing her up. She was an average height woman so she'd be able to fit into any of our cars. But before I dragged her all over the dealership, I needed to know if he had a budget. "How much are you willing to spend?" I asked the guy.

"Just show her whatever car she wants." He instructed me.

"Follow me." I said and headed in the right wing of the dealership.

Immediately after we entered in the room where we housed our Ferraris, Brian pointed out the red convertible. "Oh yeah, let's check the red one out." He suggested. He acted more excited than she did.

I watched as Brian and his girlfriend Lizette walked towards the red Ferrari. "Get behind the wheel and let me see how you look," he encouraged him. She followed his instructions and sat in the driver's seat.

"How much is this?" he asked.

"A little over two hundred thousand."

"Wow! That's a big price tag." He said while he looked at every inch of the interior.

"It may be, but it's worth it." I interjected.

"I like it. So are you going to get it for me?" she asked him.

"Yeah, if you want it."

"Okay. So, it's settled. I'm gonna take this one."
She told me.

"Sounds great. So, let's start on the paperwork."
I commented and led them back to my office. Halfway to my office Lizette asked me where the ladies
room was. After I pointed her into the right direction
she walked off while Brian followed me.

"How are you going to be paying for his?" I
asked him after he and I took a seat.

"She has the cash in her handbag." He said.

I was taken aback by his answer. Who walks
around with over $200k in their pockets? But I
didn't say it to him. I have a way of making people
look stupid after I ask them certain questions, so I let
him slide. Besides, I wanted the sale to go through.
"You know I'm not gonna be able to take your cash."
I finally said.

"Why not? I've given cash to other car sales-
men." He replied.

"I can't take anything over five grand in cash
without you filling out a lot of paperwork. I mean, if
you want to fill out the tax docs, we can move forward right now." I explained.

"Well, I'm not in the mood to be filling out a
whole bunch of paperwork so I guess we can do it
the other way."

"Who's name is the car going in?" I wanted to
know.

"It's going in her name."

"What's her full name?"

"Lizette Garcia."

"Do you know her address?" I continued to question him.

"Of course I do. We live together." He laughed. "But if you wanna move in too, I'm sure we can make room for you." He continued his humor.

"Trust me, I'm not your type." I replied sarcastically.

He reached his hands across the desk and grabbed my hand. "Oooh, your hands are so soft." He commented.

I pulled my hand from his grip. "Can we please focus?" I said. His flirtatious ways were turning me off.

"Come on, don't be a grouch. I'm only trying to be nice." He said and reached out to grab my hand again.

Thankfully his fucking girlfriend saw it. "Oh so now you're trying to fuck her too, huh?" she snapped.

"I was only trying to sweet talk her into giving us a discount on the car." He said. I looked at that nigga like he was fucking crazy. He was lying and I wanted her to know it. "First of all, you really need to tell her the truth because we don't give out discounts around here. If you couldn't afford to buy her a $200,000 car then you should've gone somewhere else like a Toyota dealership." I spat. I even stood up from my chair. I wanted this nigga to know that he was playing with the wrong sister.

He stood up from his chair too. "Bitch who the fuck you think you're talking to? I bury bitches like you who try to disrespect me and my money." He roared. He acted like he was about to hit me. So, I backed away from my desk. I wasn't about to give him room to swing at me.

"Nigga, I wish you would put your hands on me. Now get the hell out of my office witcha' low budget ass!" I warned him.

Instead of leaving my office, this nigga lunged at me with his fist. I couldn't believe my eyes. In all the time I worked here, I've never had a customer to swing on me. Was I in over my head at this place?

"Bitch, my man ain't low budget! So, get your fucking facts straight." She blurted out in an attempt to take up for her man.

"Why don't you take your man and leave my office right now before I call security." I threatened.

"Call 'em you stupid ho!" he dared me.

"Jason I need some help in here." I yelled.

"Come on baby, let's get out of here before I beat that bitch's ass!" Lizette said while she grabbed ahold of her man's hand.

By the time Jason arrived at the entryway of my office they'd exited the building. "Is everything all right?" he asked me.

I let out a loud sigh. "You will not believe what just happened." I commented and then I sat back down in my seat. I told Jason what transpired between that couple and myself and he couldn't believe it himself. "You're gonna have to be careful Kira. There are a lot of crazy people walking around these streets."

"Don't remind me." I replied.

The rest of my workday went smoothly. I talked to Dylan twice and I refused to mention what happened with me and that insane couple from earlier. I couldn't give him any ammunition to further his cause for trying to get me to quit my job. Other than what happened with those psychos, I love what I do. My new life here in Florida is great! And I wouldn't change it for the world.

I Have No Idea What's Going On

Dylan and I were lying in the bed talking about how he finally got a chance to run up on Bruce. "Where did you see him? And what did you do?" I asked while I fluffed my pillow. I wanted to give him my undivided attention.

"Sonya went back over there today so she could check on mama. And while she was there she said that nigga snuck in the house from the back door to avoid me. So, I got in my whip and hauled ass over there while Sonya was still there so she could keep mama from getting in the middle of it."

"Well, what did you do?"

"When I got there he was hiding in the room so I made that nigga unlock the door and told him to step into the living room so we could have a man to man talk."

"Did he do it?"

"He didn't have a choice."

"Did you hit 'em?"

"Yeah, I grabbed him by his neck and tried to choke the life out of him after he lied to me about putting his hands on my mama."

"What did he say?"

"He told me the same bullshit my mama said about her trying to change the light bulb and falling off the ladder."

"And what did you say?"

"I told him that if I saw another bruise on her it would be in his best interest to leave town because I was going to kill him."

"What was your mama doing when all of this was happening?"

"She tried to pull my hands from his neck and when that wasn't working she tried to get between us."

"What was Sonya doing?"

"She kept telling mama to stay out of it. But you know my mama, she's stubborn so she wasn't leaving Bruce in that room until I was gone."

"I know she's gonna be mad at you for at least a week." I pointed out. But before Dylan could respond my cell phone started ringing. I looked at the caller I.D. and saw that it was my father. I answered it on the second ring. "Hey dad, what's up?" I asked.

"Hey baby, remember when you asked me about my Judge friend Mahoney?"

"Yeah, why?" I said. But I really didn't want to know why. I just said it out of mere courtesy.

"I just got a call from his wife saying that he's missing and she doesn't no where he could be." My father replied. The tone of his voice sent me a clear message that he was extremely worried about his friend. And from that moment, I felt a huge amount of guilt because of it.

"How long has he been missing?" I asked him. I needed answers. But at the same time I was hoping that Judge Mahoney ran off with a mistress or something.

"She said he left this morning to run a few errands but he never returned."

"Has she tried to call him?" I probed my dad for more answers.

"Of course she has. I've tried calling him a few times as well."

"Well, just think positive. And I'm sure he'll show up before the night is over." I replied. I needed to give my dad hope that he'd see Judge Mahoney again. I was even crossing my fingers too, hoping for a miracle. I just pray that this is just a big miss understanding.

"Let's pray that he does." My father agreed.

"Call me, if you hear something else." I insisted.

"Sure thing." He said and then we disconnected our call.

"What was that all about?" Dylan asked me the moment I hung up with my father.

"Well, my dad got a call from his friend's wife telling him that his friend is missing. So, now he's worried that something could be wrong."

"How old is the guy?"

"I think he's in his sixties."

"Oh he's not that old. He probably got himself a little chick on the side. Call his wife and tell her that he'll come back home when he's done running the street." Dylan joked.

I punched him in the arm. "Stop it. It's not funny." I said because I knew that there was a grim chance that if Kendrick was behind Judge Mahoney's disappearance then he wasn't going home.

After Dylan and I talked a little bit more, he turned over and went to sleep. I laid there wallowing in guilt. And in the back of my mind I knew I should not have given Kendrick that man's home address. Was I that naïve to think that Kendrick wasn't going to hurt him? Shit, I knew the game. And now because of my wrong doings that man was probably dead. How the fuck am I going to clear my conscience from this?

The Following Day

I woke up the following day with my stomach in knots. I tried to convince myself that Judge Mahoney's disappearance was one big nightmare but when my father called me a couple hours later, I knew that I was not dreaming.

I had just gotten out of the shower when my dad called me. He seemed more worried than the night before. "I just got off the phone with Mahoney's wife. She said she just left the police department from filing a missing person's report."

"So, he still hasn't gone home?" I replied. I acted as if I was shocked by the news.

"No. And his wife is worried sick." My father expressed.

I wanted so badly to tell him that there was a strong possibility that Judge Mahoney disappeared at the hands of Kendrick. But I couldn't bring myself to do it. I mean, what if I was wrong? I'd be fucked. But then again, what if I was right? Kendrick would have me killed. So what was I to do? I think staying away from this mystery was the best thing for me and that was what I'd done.

"I told Mahoney's wife that you had just asked about him." My father continued.

My heart nearly jumped out of my chest when my father told me he told Mahoney's wife that I asked about him. What made him do that? Was he losing his fucking mind? My initial reaction was to curse him out but I decided against it. My dad would have a fucking heart attack if I disrespected him in any way. More importantly, he'd become very suspicious of my sudden outburst. So, in the end, I played it cool and acted like everything was okay. I was also curious as to what she had to say after my dad told her I had just asked about her husband? My father gave me this long and drawn out answer. "She only commented about how coincidental it was for you to ask about him."

"Well did you tell her how I was encouraging you to hang out with him a little more?" I interjected.

"No, that part of the conversation didn't happen."

I became irritated with my father's answer. "Why didn't your tell her that?"

"Because it wasn't the appropriate time. She doesn't want to hear about how you encouraged me to play more golf with the guy. She wants to be consoled honey." He explained. "And why are you so uptight with all of this?" My dad questioned me.

I became frozen. I didn't know how to answer his question. Was I supposed to lie? Or was I supposed to tell him the truth? "I'm not uptight daddy." I finally had the nerve to open my mouth.

"So, why are you so snappy with me?" his questions continued.

"I'm sorry daddy. I've been having some hectic days at work so please forgive me for snapping on you. Especially with everything that's going on right now."

"Okay. I accept your apology. But don't let anyone stress you out baby. Life is too precious for that."

"I won't daddy."

"All right. Well, get some sleep and I'il call you tomorrow if I hear something." He assured me.

"Okay."

Telling More Damn Lies

My father has completely stressed me the fuck out. Why the hell did he find it necessary to tell Judge Mahoney's wife that I asked about her husband? That lady didn't need to know that. Was it even necessary? This man has literally lost his damn mind. Does he realize that the fucking police may be involved now? When they suspect that there's a possible kidnapping or foul play involved in a disappearance, the police tap every phone that the victim's family has. So, by him telling that lady all that bullshit, the police could have all of that recorded.

My nerves were a complete wreck. I couldn't keep still so I paced the floor in my bedroom at least one hundred times. Finally after ten minutes of non-stop walking, I got back in bed. I was too afraid to turn on the news for the fear of hearing about Judge Mahoney. My heart wouldn't be able to handle it. That didn't stop Dylan from doing it. Five minutes after I got back in bed he came in the room carrying a hot cup of my favorite tea in his hands, turned on the TV, then he got in bed with me and handed me the mug. I didn't feel like drinking anything but he made me do it anyway. After several sips of the hot tea I became a little more at ease. "What time are you going in today?" he asked me.

"I'm not going in at all." I replied after I swallowed another cup of tea.

"What's the occasion?" he asked sarcastically.

I gave him the evil eye. "Don't play with me. I'm tired and all I want to do today is stay in the bed all day and rest. I lied. I wasn't tired. I was scared of the inevitable.

He smiled. "Okay. I'm feeling that answer. So, I guess that means I'm not doing anything today either."

"No, you don't have to stay home today because I'm staying home. I'm fine. So, go and handle whatever business you have to take care of." I insisted.

"But, I want to." He pressed the issue.

"Dylan, I don't want to hurt your feelings baby, but I just want to be alone. I'm gonna turn off my cell phone and lay in the bed all day without any interruptions."

"Okay. You can do that. I won't mess with you. But, I'm still gonna stick around just in case you wanna do something." He said, winking his eyes.

I slapped him on the arm. "You are not getting any booty today." I told him.

"That's what you think." He said as he crawled off the bed. "I'm gonna be in my man cave if you need me." He continued as he exited the bedroom.

I didn't realize that Dylan hadn't turned off the TV until he left the room. Luckily I had the remote within my reach and turned it off myself. I also turned off my cell phone. I didn't want to hear any-thing more about Judge Mahoney. I was already at my wits end. Getting another call about him would send me over the edge and I can't have that.

Time seemed to travel in slow motion. Every time I looked at the time on my cable TV box, It looked like time was at a standstill. I swear I needed this day to be over. But what I really needed was for me to snap my fingers and be gone just like that.

I finally turned the TV back on a few hours later. Dylan joined me with a pizza he ordered. We snacked on it and watched a movie he rented from the Redbox. Once the movie was over, he tried to get me to make love to him but I couldn't get in the mood. That shit with Judge Mahoney and my father took full control of my existence at this point. I couldn't function to save my life. Dylan had to feed me a slice of the pizza because I couldn't think straight. He asked me a few times if something was bothering me, but I continued to act like I was fine. I knew that he didn't believe me so I wondered how long was I going to continue on with this lie.

Sending a Message

The very next day I got up the gumption to go back to work. My father called me twice but I sent both of his calls to voicemail. I didn't want to hear anything else about Judge Mahoney. I wasn't about to incriminate myself by talking to my dad about his friend. He tricked me up once. But I refuse to let him do it again.

My day was going well. I sold a Lamborghini and I put two of my customers in leased vehicles. So, when two guys walked into my office wanting to test-drive a Bentley GT, I was a willing participant. Both men were black. One resembled the rapper Lil Wayne while the other one resembled the rapper 2-Chainz. They didn't have on a lot of jewelry but the diamond Audemar Piguet timepieces they were wearing said a lot about them. After I introduced myself, they introduced themselves. The Lil Wayne look-a-like told me his name was John and the 2-Chainz look-a-like told me his name was Chris. "Did anyone refer you?" I started the conversation as we left the lobby to search inventory in one of our exclusive showrooms.

"Yeah, one of our homeboys told us about you."
Chris said.

"What's his name?" I wondered aloud.

"We call him Andre'." Chris replied.

"Andre', umm?" I said, while I was jogging my memory.

"That's his street name. I think his wife was the one who got the car in her name." Chris continued to explain.

But for the life of me I couldn't place that name with a face so I dropped the subject. All I needed to be concerned about was servicing my new customers so I could take a nice sum of cash home. Whoever this Andre was, I sure appreciated the referral. Now if I ever find out who he was, I'd send him a Christmas card.

"So, who's buying the car?" I asked as soon as we entered into the showroom.

"I'm getting it." The Lil Wayne look-a-like said.

"John is it, right?"

"Yeah,"

"Is there any particular color you're interested in?" I asked.

John looked around the showroom floor and pointed at the black Bentley with white leather interior. "I like that one right there." He told me.

"Okay, well give me a second and I'll get the key." I said and left them standing in the middle of the floor while I fetched the car keys from the lock box on the other side of the room. Immediately after

I removed the key from the box I headed back to where the guys were standing. "Ready," I asked.

Both men nodded.

"Okay John, I'm gonna need your driver's license." I told him and held my hand out so he could give it to me.

"What are you going to do with it?" he asked me. He seemed reluctant to give it to me.

I smiled. I knew he was a dope boy so I wanted to make him feel okay about giving me his driver's license. I wanted him to know that he could trust me. "Well normally when any salesperson is going out on a test drive, we're required to make a copy of the driver's license. But since you were referred to me, I won't take a copy of your driver's license. But I am gonna have to hold on to it. I'll put it right here in my pants pocket." I told him.

"A'ight," he said.

Once I had his driver's license in my possession, I led both men to the back parking lot where we housed 90% of our inventory. After I disarmed the unlock keypad I climbed into the passenger side seat while John got into the driver seat and Chris climbed into the backseat. "Let's buckle up you guys." I said. But by the time we got on the road John was the only one that listened.

Free to move around in the back seat Chris moved to the center of the backseat and complimented every inch of the interior of the car. He also leaned forward to get a look at the front interior of the car while we exited the parking lot of the dealership. "The leather in this car is nice." He said.

"Yes, it's the top of the line. And it's imported." I commented.

"Does it come in all the Bentleys?" John wanted to know.

"Yes it does." I told him and then I abruptly changed the subject. "Keep straight to the next traffic light and then make a right so we can hop on the expressway." I instructed him.

John did as I instructed him and made the right at the next light. As we merged onto the highway I heard a click sound and before I could flinch Chris jammed the barrel of a gun to my head. I froze immediately. "What's going on? What are you doing?" I was petrified. I was afraid to move for fear of the gun going off.

"Shut the fuck up and listen to what we got to say." Chris roared. I couldn't see his face, but something inside of me told me that this was more than a test drive and that I was about to go on the ride of a lifetime.

"Do you hear me?" Chris roared again. I could hear his teeth grinding with each word he uttered.

"Yes, I hear you," I finally said.

"Good. Now listen to what I have to say because I am only going to say it once."

"Okay."

"Kendrick wants you to know that if anyone comes to you with questions about your friend Judge

Mahoney, you tell them that you don't know anything."

"Okay. Okay. I can do that."

"Good, because John and I don't want to come back to this side of town to see you again. So be a good girl and keep your mouth closed and you'll live for a very long time. But if you do the opposite, things will fall apart for you and your family. Do I make myself clear?"

"Yes. I'm clear." I said. I was a nervous fucking wreck. At this point I was willing to say anything to be able to get out of this car alive.

While Chris tormented me with the gun to my head I thought about how I fucked my life up this quick. I didn't ask for this shit. I don't want to run around Miami looking over my fucking shoulders. And I also didn't want to put my father in harms way. He had nothing to do with my decision to rat Judge Mahoney out. So, to implicate him wasn't right.

The drive back to the dealership seemed like it took forever. John didn't utter one word the entire drive. He avoided eye contact with me too. And when we pulled into a parking space in the back parking lot, he got out of the car and walked away from the car without saying goodbye. Chris didn't say another word either. He did place his finger against his mouth in an attempt to tell me to keep my mouth closed. Still shaken and horrified I nodded my head in attempt to let him know that I intended to do just that.

Finally after both of them left the dealership I raced past my office and made a beeline to the women's restroom. Thankfully no one was in there so I was alone. I looked in the mirror to see if that guy left a bruise on my face from the gun. I searched every inch of my face and found a small bruise near my left ear. It wasn't big enough to see from afar so I was lucky in that sense.

My heart was still beating uncontrollably. I couldn't get those guys out of my head. And the thought that that guy could've blown my head off terrified me. Now how the hell am I going to come back from that? I can't work anymore today. My mind is completely frazzled. I wouldn't be any help to any potential customers the way I feel right now. So, the best thing for me to do is take the rest of the day off.

I grabbed my iPad, my handbag and my car keys and headed for the exit. On my way out I told Carl that I wasn't feeling good and that I was taking off the rest of the day. He gave me the green light and told me to get well. After we made that quick exchange, I got in my car and headed home.

I've Got To Keep My Cool

Dylan wasn't home when I got there, which was a good thing so I poured myself a cold glass of wine and settled down on the chaise in my living room. I wanted to watch one of the episodes of Love & Hip Hop but I couldn't focus. It turned out that the show ended up watching me.

Once I downed my glass of wine I rested my head on one of the sofa pillows. I tried to take a nap but my eyes wouldn't close. I couldn't stop thinking about that ambush I was put in earlier. Kendrick really did a number on me when he ordered those guys to come to my job and threaten my life. And to hear that guy Chris insinuate that Judge Mahoney was dead instantly made me sick to my stomach and I knew that I was next. Normally when you hear about someone's death, nine times out of ten, you're told that because you're next in line to be executed. Kendrick had a team of niggas that would do anything for him. I was once apart of that team. But now I see that I am expendable. Dylan would call me naïve and he'd probably go upside my head because he warned me about Kendrick. He has said it for a dozen times about how fucked up Kendrick was. His heart was so cold. And to have me think that he had my back was a slap in the face. This guy made a damn mockery out of me. I was the fool and I admit it. Now I needed to figure out how I intended to keep my father and I alive. I knew I would need him to stop talking about Judge Mahoney over the phone but that wasn't it. I also needed to stop him from talking to Judge Mahoney's wife. If my dad would shut his mouth long enough, we'd probably come out of this thing in one piece.

Dylan came home about an hour later. He kissed me on my forehead and asked me what was I doing home?

"I just decided to come home early since I made my quota today." I lied. Okay well technically I didn't lie because I did make my quota. So, why should I say anything more? I was a grown ass woman. I could handle myself. I mean, I've already given Chris and John my word that I wasn't going to say anything to anyone. So, in my head I was going to be all right.

"Have you eaten?" he asked me.

"No,"

"Are you hungry?"

"Not really." I said. I really wasn't in the mood to eat anything. My nerves were shot to hell. All I wanted to do was snap my fingers and make everything go away.

"Well, I'm gonna order some Chinese. And if you want some you can heat it up and eat it later."

"Okay." I replied nonchalantly. I didn't want to talk about food. Shit I had just had a freaking gun shoved in the side of my head so food was the last thing on my mind.

"Let me ask you something." Dylan said as he stood up in front of me.

"What's up?"

"The question is, what's up with you? You haven't been yourself these last few days. So, I'm kind of wondering are you okay?"

I lifted my head up a little bit and gave him a half smile. I had to come off like I was okay. If I didn't Dylan would nag me until I told him what was really wrong with me. "Baby I am fine."

"Well, I've noticed that you've been doing a lot of laying around the apartment so I was wondering if something was going on that you aren't telling me." He replied, giving me an inquisitive facial expression. "Maybe a baby?" he blurted out.

I gave Dylan another half smile. "No, I am not pregnant silly."

"Well, can you blame me for asking. I mean you have been doing a lot of resting."

"That's because when I'm at work I'm busting my butt off all day."

"Yeah, yeah, yeah, feed someone else that mess 'cause I've gotta' use the bathroom." he said and took off in the direction of the hall bathroom.

While Dylan was handling his man duties my home phone began to ring. I reached for the cordless phone and looked at the caller I.D. and noticed that it was my father calling me. I had this eerie feeling that he'd try to get in touch with me through my house phone since I turned the ringer off on my cell phone. I held the cordless phone in my hand until it stopped ringing.

Dylan walked back into the living room while he was zipping his pants back up. "Who was that?" he asked.

"It was my dad." I replied.

"Why didn't you answer it? It might've been important, especially since he called the house phone. Normally he'll call your cell phone."

"I'm sure he has called my cell phone but I turned it off. So, that's probably why he called the house."

"Why do you have your phone off?"

"Because I don't feel like being bothered."

"Wow! That's a new one for me. You never turn your phone off." He replied sarcastically.

"Well, I'm doing it now." I told him. I was being a smartass just like he was.

"Don't ignore the guy. He may wanna talk to you about his friend. Did they find him yet?" Dylan questioned me.

"I'm not sure."

"Come on now Kira, don't leave the man hanging like that. Answer his call. You're probably the only person he can talk to right now."

"He's got other buddies that he can call. I just don't want him to pound my head about his judge friend. I don't like hearing about bad things happening to people."

"Who said something bad happened to him?"

Oh my God! Did I just blow my whole cover? Why did I say that something bad happened to Judge Mahoney? Oh boy, Dylan is going to give me the third degree now.

"I'm not saying something bad happened. I'm just saying, I don't want to keep hearing about other people's business. I've got a lot of crap on my own plate." I managed to say. I'm going to have to be more careful about what I say out of my mouth. I almost blew my cover in front of Dylan.

"Never mind all of that. You know your pops needs you right now so give 'em a call after you rest up."

"I will." I said. But in the back of my mind I knew I wasn't going to call my father back. I just needed to get him off my back.

Right after Dylan left the room I turned the ringer off on the home phone. Dylan never used the house phone so I knew I'd be in the clear with that. I even turned the ringer off on the kitchen and bedroom phones too. I had to make sure I covered all bases. When I finally got up the nerve to call my father it would be on my terms. Better yet, I figured it would better suit me and my father if I visit him in person, that way the cops won't have me on any recordings. I've got to stay on these streets as long as I can. I also had to look out for my father because he's not familiar with this lifestyle. In other words, I'd die first before I let anything happen to him.

The Perfect Set-up

I hadn't realized it but I had dozed off on the sofa for about forty-five minutes. Unfortunately for me that was all the rest I got. Dylan chose to wake me up nearly scaring the cramp out of me. "Baby, your father is on the phone. He says it's an emergency. I jumped up semi-incoherent but I was still able to take his cell phone after he shoved it in my hand. "Hello," I said, still a little groggy."

"Kira, what's wrong with your phones? I've being trying to call you all day." My father yelled through the phone.

"I was taking a nap dad. What's the matter?"

"They found Judge Mahoney." He yelled.

I sat straight on the sofa. "What do you mean they found him? Is he okay?" I forced myself to say. Knowing that I had just had Kendrick's boys threaten my life earlier, I knew I couldn't say much over the phone.

"No baby, my friend is dead." My father said. His voice sounded sad and heavy.

"Calm down daddy and tell me what's going on?"

While I was waiting for my father to give me more details about Judge Mahoney, Dylan had taken a seat on the sofa next to me so he could hear our conversation. I was somewhat uncomfortable by him sitting there next to me, but I let it roll off my back. I figured if I got my dad to cut this conversation short we would both be in a win-win situation. I didn't have to worry about Dylan drilling me with questions or have my dad say too much for the fear that someone else could be listening. Things would definitely turn for the worse very quick. "Homicide detectives just left Mahoney's home and told his wife that they just found his body."

"Daddy listen, don't say another word. I'm getting ready to get into my car and head over to your house right now. So, I'll see you in about fifteen minutes. Okay?" I told him.

"Okay," he replied.

I ended our call and handed Dylan the phone as I stood up to my feet. "Are you going to be good driving over to your pop's crib by yourself?" he asked me.

"Yes, I'm gonna be fine. I'll call you when I'm on my way back to the house." I assured him.

"A'ight. Make sure you do that." He said.

It didn't take me long at all to slide on a pair of sneakers and grab my handbag. Before I left the apartment, I called valet and asked for them to have my car waiting out front.

On the way to my father's house I felt on edge and scared that someone may be following me, especially after knowing what my father just told me. With each streetlight I went through I looked over my shoulders. I was a nervous wreck the entire time while I drove to my father's house. I thought I was built for this life. But I wasn't. I just want a simply life, one that kept me off the radar when it came to dealing with cats like Kendrick. At the end of the day I needed to figure out a way to steer my father from this incident dealing with Judge Mahoney. I knew he was a great friend to my father but Judge Mahoney was a shady nigga. He had to be if Kendrick came to me to find out where he lived. So, whether my father likes it or not, he has to distance himself. If not, then things are going to get ugly pretty fast.

By the time I reached my father's house my heart had settled in the pit of my stomach. I didn't have the nerve or the energy to get out of my car but after sitting behind the wheel for a minute and a half I managed to talk myself into doing it.

My father must've heard my car when I drove up. He looked distraught and he looked like he hadn't had any sleep in the last couple of days. He grabbed me into his arms after he let me into the house. "I'm so glad you're here," he said and then he closed and locked the front door.

I grabbed his hand and escorted him to the family room. We both took a seat on the sofa near the TV.

He had it locked on the news channel so I figured he was looking for more news surrounding Judge Mahoney's murder.

"So tell me everything that's going on?" I didn't hesitate to say after we sat down.

"Well, I got a call from Mahoney's wife a few hours ago telling me that two homicide detectives came by her home and told her that they found Judge Mahoney."

"Where?"

"She told me they found him shot and burned to death inside of his car."

"What do you mean shot and burned?" I asked.

"Kira, whoever killed him shot him in his head and then they doused the car with gasoline and set it on fire while he was in it." My father said, this time with tears in his eyes.

My heart couldn't stand seeing my father like this so I reached over and started rubbing his back in a circular motion. "Daddy, please don't cry. Everything's gonna be alright." I told him, even though I didn't believe it myself.

I knew what type of nigga we were dealing with. I just wished that I'd listened to Dylan when he told me not to fuck with Kendrick. But now it's too late. We still have to move forward.

"Do you know the police also found partially burned one hundred dollar bills shoved inside of his mouth?"

"Oh my God! Really!?" I replied. I thought of Kendrick shoving money down Judge Mahoney's throat before they set him on fire to send out a clear message that Judge Mahoney made someone very unhappy. Now I see why Kendrick sent his boys up to the dealership. They knew that I would soon find out about his murder, so they felt it very necessary to warn me about opening my mouth. Their point was well taken.

"I vow that whoever did that to my friend will pay heavily. They will get the death penalty after I'm done with them." My father cried.

"Daddy you're gonna have to calm down and let the police handle their investigation." I said. I really want him to back off for the sake of his own life.

While my father continued to talk about Judge Mahoney's death, someone rang the doorbell. It shocked the hell out of me. Paranoid by the untimely visitor, I asked my father if he was expecting anyone. After he told me he wasn't I immediately got an uneasy feeling. One part of me wanted to run out the backdoor and the other part of me wanted to hide somewhere in the house. Either way, I wanted to avoid opening the door.

Without saying another word my father left me in the family room to see who was at the door. I sat there quietly hoping that whoever was at the front door wasn't here to hurt me or my father. "Yes, come on in the back. My daughter is here with me and we were talking about what happened." I heard my father say.

I had no idea who he was talking to until he resurfaced with two white plain- clothes detectives. Seeing them standing before me made me feel intimidated. "Kira, this is Detective Grimes and Detective Lowes."

Both detective extended their hands and shook mine. "Nice to meet you." I said, trying to look perfectly normal. I've heard stories about how cops can read body language so I wanted to appear confident.

"Have a seat gentlemen." My father said.

Both detectives sat in chairs opposite of the sofa my dad and I were sitting on. "Can I offer you men something to drink?" My father asked.

"No, we're fine. But thank you," said one of the men.

"Well, what can I do for you guys?" My father wanted to know.

"Mrs. Mahoney gave us your name and thought that you might be able to provide us with some information about Mr. Mahoney's last days that led up to his murder." One of the detectives said while he pulled out a small notepad and an ink pen from the inside of his suit jacket.

"Well, all I can tell you is that he and I talked quite a bit about getting together to play golf. But that's about it."

"When was this?" the same detective asked.

"About three days ago."

"So, was that the last time you spoke with him?" the detective continued to question my father.

I noticed the other detective watching me while his partner questioned my father. This guy was making me feel so uneasy. I held my composure, though.

"Yes, that was the last time I spoke to him?"

"Now I was told that you and Mr. Mahoney worked together. So, while you and he were presiding on the bench did you see him make any enemies?"

"Come on detective, he and I have given out some long prison terms to some very dangerous men so of course we've made some enemies along the way."

"Well, did he have any enemies outside of his courtroom?"

"Not to my knowledge."

"Do you think he was involved in any illegal activities?"

"Of course not. What kind of question is that? Judge Mahoney was an upstanding judge. Everyone in our court system respected him." My father spat. He quickly became upset at the mention of Judge Mahoney doing something bad.

"You do know that there was money found stuffed in his mouth?"

"Yes I am. And when I find out who did that despicable act against him they will pay. I'm going to make sure they rot in jail."

"Can you tell us how Mr. and Mrs. Mahoney's relationship was?"

"I'm sure it was great."

"So, he's never mentioned that he was having problems in his marriage and that he wanted to get a divorce?"

"No. As far as I understand he loved her."

"What about you? How was your relationship with him?"

"Our relationship was great. We were more like brothers than friends."

"Can you tell us where you were on the night he was killed?"

I could tell he was getting tired of answering the detective's questions. The fact that this clown wanted to know my father's whereabouts during the time period of which Judge Mahoney was killed offended him. My father wasn't the fucking killer! I wanted to tell these clowns to get the hell out of here. For a moment, it looked like my father wanted to tell them to take a hike too. Thankfully the detective backed off after my father gave them his alibi.

What the detective did next shocked my father and I. "Did you know Judge Mahoney?" the cop asked me.

I did a double take. This question came out of the blue. It also had taken me aback. I didn't know that man personally. So, why the fuck is this guy coming for me? "Are you talking to me?" I asked sarcastically. I even rolled my eyes in a gesture to let him know that I was offended.

"Yes, I am." The detective replied. He looked me straight into my eyes.

"Well to answer your question, no I didn't know him. He was my father's friend. Not mine." I told him. My voice was stern and I was direct.

"Mrs. Mahoney said that she and Mr. Mahoney has come here for barbecues and dinners and that she's seen you interact with her husband. So are you still saying that you don't know him?"

"Look officer, I've talked to a lot of people that my father has invited into this house but that doesn't mean that I know them." I snapped. This white guy was getting on my fucking nerves. He was barking up the wrong tree. "Now, I'm gonna excuse myself." I told him. Then I turned my attention back to my father. "Dad, I'm going home. But if you need anything call me." I said and then I let myself out.

My ride back home wasn't a pleasant one. I couldn't stop thinking about how those cops were interrogating me and my father. We didn't kill Judge Mahoney, so they needed to get their fucking facts straight. I just hoped I did the right thing by leaving my father at the house with those thirsty ass detectives. My father had a history of talking too much. I only hoped that he'd say the right things and be careful not to let those crackers know that I asked him where Judge Mahoney lived. I strongly believed that if he did, those cops were going to find a way to drag me into their investigation. I guess now is the time for me to get down on my knees and pray for the best.

Decisions

Dylan wasn't home when I returned from my father's house. I called him after I had taken off my clothes and gotten in the bed. "Hey baby, where are you?" he asked me.

"Yeah, I just got back."

"So how is your dad?"

"He's doing okay for the moment." I lied. My father was really a nervous fucking wreck. But I didn't feel like explaining everything that went on. "So, when are you coming home?" I changed the subject.

"In a couple of hours."

"Alright, well drive careful and I'll see you later." I told him.

"Okay, baby."

I got up the next morning and decided to call off again. I told my boss Carl that I was still feeling a little under the weather. I also told him that I planned to take some additional days off so I was going to use some of the vacation time. "Get better." He told me.

Now that I had gotten my vacation time approved I knew I could relax a little. I really needed to find a way to move forward with a clear conscious about Judge Mahoney's murder. The only people who knew that I gave up Judge Mahoney's whereabouts was Kendrick, his bodyguard and those other two guys that Kendrick sent up to the dealership to put fear in me.

I felt all alone knowing that I had no one in my corner. I wanted to tell Dylan what happened after I opened my mouth and because of it my father's friend is dead, but I had no idea how Dylan would take that information.

One part of me feared that he'd leave me and then I'd really be screwed. And the other part of me feared that Dylan would confront Kendrick and then a war would break out, causing a lot of people to be killed. I didn't want that to happen so I figured the best thing for me to do would be to try to handle things myself.

Maybe if my dad would remain neutral and stop talking to Mrs. Mahoney and the police this whole thing could blow over. Hopefully my wish will come true and no one else would get hurt.

Because Dylan was out so late the night before he didn't get up until around 12 noon. He came into the living room where I was surfing the internet from my iPad. "I knew I heard you in here." He smiled.

I let out a long sigh. "Yeah, I decided to take another day off."

"That's good because we need to talk." He said as he took a seat on the sofa next to me.

I took my eyes off the iPad for a moment to search Dylan's face. The fact that he wanted to talk to me ruffled my feathers a little. Normally when he says he wants to talk, nine times out of ten the topic is serious. So, I braced myself. "What's up?" I forced myself to say. I knew he wanted to ask me questions about Judge Mahoney's murder and I didn't want to go there right now.

"While I was out last night, I got word from some people I deal with saying that judge that got killed because he got paid three hundred grand to dismiss a couple of cases. Apparently he skipped out on them. Turns out those nigga found out where he lived and did him in."

"Did they say who did it?" I wanted to know.

"They said it was Kendrick's people."

"Really?" I said, in a shocking manner.

"Yes, really." He replied.

It always amazed me how quickly the streets got information. The streets stayed talking. But did they mention how Kendrick found out where the judge lived? I was too afraid to ask Dylan that question so I passed.

"So what's going on with your father? How is he dealing with his friend getting killed?"

"He's taking it really hard. He's actually taking this thing too personal. While I was there yesterday two homicide cops stopped by to talk to him. So after they were done asking him questions, they started asking me questions."

"What did they ask you?"

"They wanted to know how much I knew the man. So I told them I didn't know shit about him. And that the only time I saw him was when he and his wife stopped by to see my dad."

"Stay away from that bullshit! We don't need that type of heat."

"I know. And that's why I was surprised that he would even ask me anything about that man."

"Look baby, you're gonna have to put a bug in your pops ear about that murder."

"Whatcha' mean?"

"All I'm saying is that he's gonna have to chill out with talking to the police."

"I know. I was going to talk to him about that later."

"Yeah, get on that a.s.a.p. Because those niggas that fucked that judge up like that don't play fair."

"I know." I sighed. Here I was unable to figure out what to do. Talk about decisions.

Race Against Time

For the past few days I purposely ignored my father's calls. I made up my mind that I didn't want to talk about Judge Mahoney anymore. I figured that if I shut down all communication with him he'd find someone else to talk to and finally leave me alone. Whether he knew it or not, I was doing this for the both of us. This was the best solution in my mind.

While I was in the shower Dylan burst in the bathroom hysterically. "Hey baby, you've gotta' come and see this shit." He said. He scared the fuck out of me.

"What is it?"

"Your father is on TV with some Haitian looking lady." He yelled and then he scrambled back out of the bathroom.

Once again my heart took a dive into the pit of my stomach. I grabbed a towel from the towel rack and wrapped myself in it while I raced to the living room. As soon as I walked into the room I saw my father standing behind Judge Mahoney's wife at a press conference. I was about to freak out. I couldn't believe my eyes. "What the fuck is he doing?" I said aloud.

"If anyone out there has any information that would lead to the arrest of the murderer that killed my husband so viciously please contact the local authorities because there is a $50,000 reward." Judge Mahoney's wife pleaded.

"Yes, please contact your local authorities if you have any information. We have to get this murderer off the streets. If we don't then he may kill again. So, let's do the right thing people. We're depending on you." My father stepped up to say.

"Wow! You're pops is brave. You may want to call him on his cell phone right now and tell 'em he needs to back off." Dylan warned me.

I continued to stand there in disbelief. What the fuck was wrong my father? He was taking this shit to another level.

"Are you gonna call him or what?" Dylan pressed the issue.

"Yes, I'm going to call him." I sucked my teeth and stormed off. I went into my bedroom so I could dry off and put on some clothes.

Dylan got up from the chair and followed me. "Look, I'm not trying to add more stress to you. But this shit could get serious."

"Don't you think I know that?" I snapped. I just wanted Dylan to shut up. Everything he was about to tell me, I already knew.

"Do you know that none of my partners know that your father was a judge?"

"You've told me that already." I said sarcastically.

"Well, nip that shit in the bud and I won't say nothing else about it."

"Good," I snapped and then I left him in our bedroom.

Struggling With The Truth

Seeing my father at a press conference with Judge Mahoney's wife was the last fucking straw for me. I knew he cared for and respected Judge Mahoney but there still needs to be a limit to shit you'd do for people. That man stole money from the wrong people. It was simple as that. So, something needs to click in my daddy's mind that Judge Mahoney had to have pissed off somebody. I mean, who shoots you in the head execution style, stuffs one hundred dollar bills in your mouth and then sets you and your car on fire? Can't they see what's going on? The fucking writing is on the wall. So they need to open their freaking eyes.

After I got on the road I pulled out my cell phone and called my father to see where he was. He answered on the third ring. "Hi baby, how are you?" he greeted me.

"We need to talk," I told him.

"Well right now isn't a good time. Can you come by the house in about an hour?"

"No daddy. We need to talk now." I demanded.

"I've been calling you for the last couple of days but you didn't return my phone calls and now you want to talk?" he replied sarcastically.

"Okay I was wrong. I should've called you. But while I've got you on the phone I need you to say that you're gonna meet up with me now." I said. I couldn't let another couple of hours go by without getting him to meet with me face to face.

My father got silent for a few seconds and then he said, "Okay, I'll agree to see you right now, but you've got to come to Mrs. Mahoney's house. This is where I'm gonna be for the next couple of hours."

"Is that where the press conference is?"

"Yes, but we just wrapped it up. The camera crew is packing up their gear as we speak."

I was reluctant to go to Mrs. Mahoney's home but then I figured that I didn't have a choice. I needed to see my father face to face if I had to meet him somewhere other than his house, then so be it.

"I'm on my way. What's the address?" I forced myself to say. After he gave me the address I keyed it in my navigation system and started my journey.

Halfway to Mrs. Mahoney's house I made a de-tour to the Wawa gas station. I needed gas really bad. Unfortunately all the pumps were occupied so I parked behind a red Chevy Charger and waited for the pump to become available. Two minutes in my cell phone rang. I looked down at the caller I.D. and noticed that the call was blocked. I nearly freaked out. Something told me that it was either Kendrick calling me, or it was his boys. Either way, I knew I shouldn't answer it.

The call rang seven times before it stopped. And immediately after it stopped I turned my ringer off. I needed to focus on getting my father back in line. So, I don't need any distractions.

Finally when the pump became available I filled up my car and then I got out of there. It took me approximately twenty minutes to get to Mrs. Mahoney's house. Anxiety sat in the pit of my stomach the entire ride there and it swallowed me whole the moment I drove onto the property. Local TV crew vans were parked on each side of the street, so I found it very hard to find a parking space. Luckily my dad saw me and hustled his way onto the street. "Sorry about the parking," he said after I rolled down the driver side window.

"It's okay. Get in." I replied.

The moment he sat down in the passenger seat of my car I went straight street mode on his ass. "Daddy, I don't want you to think that I'm about to disrespect you in any way but you're gonna have to listen to me and listen to me good." I said.

"Okay, go for what you know." He said and gave me the floor.

"Look I know you're hurt behind Judge Mahoney's death. But you can't be talking to these news reporters. You can't get involved with that daddy."

"Why can't I? He'd do it for me. And besides, Judge Mahoney was my friend Kira."

"Daddy, don't you think I know that?" I snapped.

"Well if you know that then why are we having this conversation?" he shot back.

I could tell that he was getting tired of me chastising him. But I was doing it for his own good. "Do you remember what they did to Judge Mahoney?" I got straight to the point.

"What kind of question is that? Of course, I do."

"Well don't you think that if they'd torture and set him on fire with money shoved down his throat that they'd do the same to you, especially if you're on TV telling the whole world that you're going to go to the depths to make sure they get prosecuted?"

"Do you know how many men and women I sent to prison for a long time?"

"And what does that mean?"

"It means that if I can send hard core criminals away for the rest of their lives and can still go home and sleep at night, then what makes you think that I'm gonna let some punk intimidate me? I am a retired judge Kira. I call the shots! Not you or no one else. Do you understand that?"

As much as I wanted to argue my point with my father and come clean with all the facts about who murdered Judge Mahoney, I knew he still wouldn't walk away. My father was a stubborn man. Now I see that there was nothing I could say or do that would make him change his mind. I'm starting to believe that maybe he has a death wish. Every since my mother died he hasn't been himself. Sounds like he's ready to see her again.

In total, my father and I argued for about ten minutes. And while we were talking one another's head off, I saw the silhouette of two guys sitting in a black, late model SUV with semi-tinted windows. It scared the crap out of me. I had to bring my dad's attention to it. "Daddy, don't look now but do you see two black guys sitting in the front seat of that black SUV parked six cars behind that white car?" I asked him.

My father slowly turned his head in the direction of the black SUV. A few seconds later he said, "Yes, I see it. Who do you think it is?" he asked me.

"I'm not sure. But with all the media attention over here, it could be anyone."

"Think it's the guys that killed Judge Mahoney?"

"It could be. And that's why I want you to be careful daddy. I would lose my mind if something happened to you."

"Baby girl, daddy is going to be fine." He said, simultaneously looking to see any movement from the black SUV. "Look, why don't you hurry up and get out of here and I'll call you later." He said.

"Why are you trying to rush me out of here?"

"Because I'm gonna call the cops and get them to see who those guys are and I don't want you around when they do it."

"Daddy, I don't think that that's a good idea." I advised him.

"Kira, do what I say honey and get out of here. I'll call you as soon as I get home," he instructed me and then he patted me on my thigh.

Before I could utter another word, my father had gotten out of the car and closed the door. "Get out of here now." He yelled from the outside of the car and hit the hood of my car.

Before I drove away I looked at the black SUV for a few seconds. Whoever was inside didn't flinch. The thought of them just sitting there gave me the creeps. In my mind, anyone who kills someone and hangs out around the victim's home is brave and insane. That was my cue to leave.

Staying Alive

It felt good to be back home. As soon as I pulled my car up in front of the building I hopped out and the valet guy hopped in and drove away to park it. "Back so soon," the doorman said.

I gave him a half smile. "Looks that way." I commented.

I raced to the elevator upon entering the building. I wanted so badly to walk through the front door of my apartment that I could taste it. After I pressed the button I stood there patiently and out of nowhere I heard a voice coming from behind me. "Tell your pops to chill out before he ends up like that other judge." The man's voice said.

Startled, I turned around to see who had just threatened me but by the time I looked, all I could see was the back of a black guy walking towards the front door of the lobby. "Hey, you..." I yelled but the guy wouldn't look back.

One second later the elevator door opened. I struggled with the decision to get on the elevator or follow that guy to see who he was and where he was going. But then I decided against it. I needed to get inside of my apartment where Dylan was. At least there he could provide me with some protection.

"Okay Kira, you gotta' calm down and take control of your breathing." I uttered softly, while I was fumbling with my keys. Dylan must've heard me because he pulled the door open before I could stick the key into the lock.

"Hey baby, are you okay?" he asked.

"Yeah, I'm okay." I lied as I moved by him. I dropped my handbag and keys onto the coffee table.

"Did you get a chance to talk to your father?" he asked as he stood before me.

I sighed heavily. "Yeah."

"So, what did you say to him?"

"I just told him that he's gonna have to chill out before the guys that killed his friend come after him."

"And what did he say?"

"He didn't really say anything." I lied once again. I realized that I couldn't come home and tell Dylan that my father had no intentions to stop helping the cops find out who murdered his friend. Dylan wouldn't let me live it down. He'd talk my head off for the rest of the night if he knew the truth.

"Well, does he realize that this is not his fight?"

"Yes, he does. And by the look in his face I believe he's gonna take a back seat."

"Good because money is good right now. So, starting a war with Kendrick's boys behind your pops would definitely stop my flow."

"Yeah, yeah, yeah, I know." I said.

Should've Seen This Coming

When something is racking your brain you can't function properly. Knowing that that guy stood by me at the elevator and told me to check my father and then abruptly walks away put a new degree of fear in me.

I've had niggas threaten to whip my ass in the past but to have someone put a gun to my head and then have someone come up to me where I live is crossing the line.

I tried to eat some of the tuna fish and crackers Dylan prepared for me but I couldn't. I couldn't get my mind off the press conference that my father attended with Judge Mahoney's wife. I also couldn't stop thinking about that black SUV that was parked near Mrs. Mahoney's house.

I wanted to call my father to see if the cops ever came out there and found out who the men were, but then I figured that calling him would be too risky for the fact that his phone could be tapped.

While I was playing with my plate of tuna fish and crackers Dylan approached me. "Can't get your mind off your father, huh?" he asked.

"I just wished he wasn't so stubborn sometimes." I said.

"He'll be a'ight if he'd stay in his own lane."

"I know. So, hopefully he knows it too." I replied.

"Well, look I gotta' go and meet up with Sean. So, if you need something just call me." He said and kissed me on my forehead.

"Alright." I said, as I watched him leave the apartment. When the door closed behind I instantly felt alone. I also felt vulnerable, especially since that guy was able to get into my building and sneak up behind me while I was at the elevator.

While I dragged myself out of the kitchen and into the living room to watch a little bit of TV, my cell phone rang. I immediately became numb. I was afraid of answering it for the fear that it was Kendrick or one of his boys calling me. I swear I wished that they would just leave me alone.

In total the phone rang five times and then it stopped. And when I picked it up to see who called me, the fucking thing stared ringing again. My heart sunk. But when I looked at the caller I.D. and saw that it was my father calling, I felt relieved and exhaled. "Hey daddy, what's up?" I asked.

"Kira, I need you to get over here right now!" he yelled.

The initial shock of his scream sent me into panic mode. I was feeling a multitude of emotions. "Daddy, what's wrong?" I yelled.

"Baby, I'm gonna need you to get to my house now."

"Why daddy? What's wrong? Tell me what's wrong?" I yelled. But my words fell on death ears because our call failed.

Without much hesitation I threw on a pair of sneakers, snatched my car keys from the kitchen counter and then I made a detour to my bedroom where Dylan kept his guns. I grabbed the first gun I saw, which was a 9MM Glock. I knew I couldn't make the trip to my father's house without protection. So after I made sure the magazine was filled with Dylan's special hollow-tips I put it on safety, shoved it down into the purse that was laying on my bed and then I left my apartment.

During the course of my drive I tried several times to get my father on the phone but it kept going straight to voicemail. "Daddy, what's going on? Why you ain't answering your damn phone?" I whined because so many thoughts were running through my mind. My gut told me that my father was hurt. He literally sounded like he was in agony. So, I pictured the worse case scenario, especially after seeing those two niggas casing Judge Mahoney's place. I mean, what if they got him hostage? And what if they beat him up really bad? The guy that came at me while I was waiting at the elevator warned me to tell my father to back off. So, what if they are at his house? Should I call the cops? Or should I call Dylan? I figured this thing has gone too far and he needs to know. So, what am I supposed to do?

I held my cell phone in my hand the entire drive to my father's house. I even cruised down his street to make sure I wasn't running into an ambush. Looking over my shoulders has become second nature, which wasn't a good thing. I mean who wants to be paranoid and live in fear the rest of their lives? That was not a life I wanted.

Immediately after I stopped my car, I grabbed the gun from my purse, took the safety off, dashed up the winding driveway of my father's home and made my way inside. "Daddy," I yelled as soon as I stepped over the threshold of the front door. I braced myself for what I was about to see. My heart was racing at an uncontrollable speed. "Daddy," I yelled once more.

I heard footsteps coming from behind me. When I turned to look it was my father holding a shotgun in his hands. He looked disheveled and his eyes were filled with tears.

"Daddy, are you okay? What's going on?" I asked.

"Mrs. Mahoney is dead." He said and then he fell to his knees.

With my gun held firmly in my left hand, I leaned over and hugged my father with my right hand. The last time I saw him this broken up was when my mother died.

"Daddy, I need you to get it together. We need to talk." I told him as I watched him cry.

"She didn't deserve that. We are dealing with a bunch of monsters." My father said, while he continued to sob.

It took me about three whole minutes to get him back on his feet. "Come on daddy, we gotta' get out of here." I said and led him to the front door.

"I'm taking my shotgun with me." He said matter of factly and began to wipe the tears away from his eyes.

"That's fine. But I'm gonna need your help."

He stopped in his tracks. "What is it?"

"When we go outside to go to the car, I'm gonna need you to help me look around to make sure no one is coming for us. Okay?"

"Okay," he said.

"Here we go." I commented and literally took off running to my car with my father in tow.

"Slow down baby, you know I can't run that fast." He said trying to catch his breath.

"Just hold on to your shotgun, we're almost there." I assured him while I dragged him. I felt relieved when he and I made it to the car. After I locked the door I backed my car out of his driveway and sped out of there.

My father was never a big talker, especially when it came to serious matters such as death. I stared at him through my peripheral vision and watched him look straight ahead with his shotgun placed between his knees. So, after five miles into the drive I knew I was going to have to make him talk about Mrs. Mahoney. "Daddy, how are you feeling right now?" I asked him, trying to touch the subject as gentle as I could.

"I don't know how I'm feeling. My entire body is numb." He replied.

"How did you find out that Mrs. Mahoney was dead?"

"One of the detectives that came to my house when you were there, called me with the news."

"What did he say?"

"Kira, all he said was that she was dead."

"He didn't say how she died?" I pressed the issue. I needed more answers and my father wasn't quite doing the job.

"No he didn't."

"Do you think the two guys we saw sitting in that black SUV did it?" I asked him.

"That's a huge possibility."

"Did you ever tell the cops about them?"

"Yes, I did. But by the time they arrived, the guys had already left."

"Daddy, this is scary."

"I know it is Kira. But don't you worry, I am going to handle it."

"Well, I think you should let the police do their job and stay out of it." I said. I wasn't trying to be a smart ass. I just wanted my father to know that the people that murdered Mr. and Mrs. Mahoney were mercenaries. They didn't give a damn about anyone, including their own family. But of course, my father turned a death ear. I knew it was going to take more than talking to prove to him that he needs to stay out of the way.

"Where are you taking me?" he asked, abruptly changing the subject.

"To my house. Why?"

"Because I want you to take me by the Mahoney's residence. I need to see what's going on." He said adamantly.

"No daddy, we can't go there. Do you know how dangerous that would be? We could walk right in the line of fire."

"I don't care what you say! Take me by there now." He demanded.

"Do you have a death wish or something?" I replied sarcastically.

Irritated by my hesitation to give into his demands, he snapped and said, "No I don't. But I am sick and tired of you trying to control me and tell me what to do."

"Daddy, I'm only doing it for your own good."

"Kira, I am not going to say it again. Now take me to the Mahoney's residence right now." He shot back at me. I saw the hurt in his eyes. He really wanted to drive by Mrs. Mahoney's house to see first hand what was going on.

Reluctantly I gave in to his insane demand. "Alright, fine. If you wanna go by there then I'll take you. But we're only staying there for a couple of minutes. That's all. Now do you agree?"

"Yes, that's fair." He said.

"I mean it daddy." I warned him. "We're gonna ride by there and take a quick look and then we're gonna leave okay?"

"Okay," he answered me.

The drive to the Mahoney's house took about thirty minutes to get there. For some reason the traffic was backed up. My father didn't mind, he was so fixated on going there, everything outside of that didn't mean a thing to him.

As we pulled up to the residence, we noticed that the cops had the street blocked off with the yellow tape that they rolled out to secure any evidence that would be volatile for their investigation. We also saw the coroner with Mrs. Mahoney's body zipped up inside of a black bag. "Oh my god! She's really dead." He said covering his mouth with his hand.

Before I could utter a word, he had opened the passenger side door and jumped out. "No, daddy, wait." I yelled.

He didn't stop. So, I put my car in park and got out of the car behind him. Before I could get to him, one of the cops stopped him in his tracks. "Sorry sir but I can't let you walk behind this tape." I heard the cop say.

"But, that's my friend's wife." My father began to explain.

"I'm sorry sir, but I can't let you by." The cop held his ground.

"Do you know who you're talking to son?" My father snapped.

"No sir, I don't."

"I'm retired Judge Wade. And I can have your job taken from you with one damn phone call."

"I'm sorry Judge Wade. I didn't know it was you sir." The cop replied and gave into my father's tantrum. Just like a kid in a candy store my father got his way and acted like the world revolved around him. I stood a ways back from the yellow tape. I was standing amongst a few of the Mahoney's neighbors who were all Caucasian and listened to what they had to say. There were two women and three men. "This is so sad." One of the women neighbors said.

"Yes it really is. I mean, who'd think that she'd get murdered right after her husband was killed?" the other woman commented.

"Do you think that press conference she had brought the killers back to murder her?" The first woman asked.

"It sure seems that way." One of the three elderly men said.

"Has the detectives come by to talk to any of you?" the elderly guy continued.

"I spoke with them after Mr. Mahoney was murdered." The first elderly woman said.

"Yes, I think we all have." The second woman confirmed.

"Did you hear that Mr. Mahoney was involved in some illegal activities?" the second woman continued to speak.

"Nancy Pegler who lives down the block said that she saw him having lunch at Catch 52 on the water with some guys that looked like thugs." The first woman said.

"Sounds like a drug deal gone bad if you ask me." One of the elderly men added.

"I agree," said the second woman.

I stood there and listened to those men and women as they tried to piece together the mystery behind the Mahoney murders. They had all kinds of theories but no one really knew what happened to the Mahoneys but me. Whether or not it was a gift or a curse was totally up to God. I figured all I needed to worry about was my father's safety and I was good. No harm. No foul.

"Excuse me Miss," I heard one of the elderly ladies say.

I knew she was talking to me because I was the only person that the group didn't know. I turned around to engage them. "Are you talking to me?" I asked, even though I knew my question was rhetorical.

"Yes dear," the woman replied, "are you related to the Mahoneys?" she continued.

"No ma'am. They were friends of my father. My father and Mr. Mahoney worked together as Circuit Judges for the Miami-Dade Courts."

"Oh wow! That's a pity." The same lady commented.

"Is that your father over there talking to the police detective?" one of the elderly men asked.

I turned and looked in the direction that the man was pointing to. And when I realized that he was talking about my father, I told him yes.

"Do you know if the Mahoney's have any relatives in the area?" The same lady asked. She was an inquisitive woman. She did the majority of the talking.

"I don't have any idea. But I'm pretty sure my dad knows." I told her.

I believe the neighbors had thrown at least fifty questions at me. They were on a roll. Thankfully, my father finally decided to end his own personal investigation and made his way back over to me.

He motioned for me to meet him at my car and that's what I did.

What A Bloody Mess

"You will not believe what I just saw." My father started off the conversation as I drove away from the scene.

"What was it?" I asked, sounding like I was begging.

"The detective that called me about Mrs. Mahoney pulled me to the side and showed me her body." He replied slowly. I could tell that he wanted me to hear every word clearly.

"Oh my God! How did she look?" I wanted to know.

"Whoever killed her shot her in the back five times."

"Daddy no. Really?!" I said, somewhat shocked. I mean, why shoot the lady five times? She didn't deserve that.

"Yes. The poor woman looked like she was trying to flee for her life. But those fucking savages pumped lead into her like she was an animal."

"What did the cop say about it?"

My father let out a long sigh. "He didn't talk much. I did all the talking."

"What did you say?"

"I told him that every cop in the area should be on this case. Everyone involved in the Mahoney murders need to be found by sun up. And after they are caught they need to be tortured and burned alive." My father roared. He was literally foaming at the mouth.

"Come on daddy, don't get worked up. The cops will find them." I said, with hopes of calming him down. But he ignored me.

"I'm gonna make sure they get the fucking death penalty if that's the last thing I do." He continued to roar.

While my father poured his heart out and his desire to make the murderers pay for his friends' murders, my cell phone rang. I saw it sitting in the cup holder near the gearshift so I picked it up and answered it. "Hello," I said.

"I see you didn't get my first message." The male voice said.

Immediately after I realized that the voice belonged to Kendrick I became panic-stricken and caught a sharp pain in my right side. I was afraid to speak for the fear that I would alarm my father. But Kendrick wasn't having that. He was going to have a two-way conversation whether I liked it or not.

"Do I need to make a trip over to your place of residence?" he asked sarcastically.

"No," I said, but it was barely audible.

"Well, when I ask you a fucking question bitch, you need to answer me." He snapped. I pressed my cell phone as tight as I could so I could prevent my father from hearing what Kendrick was saying.

"What message are you talking about?" I asked, even though I knew what he was talking about. It was my way of trying to calm down the mood of this conversation.

"I sent my man over to your place of residence to tell you to keep your pops on a short leash before he ends up like his friends. But I'm now starting to believe that you didn't get the memo."

"Oh yeah, I got it." I said and then I looked at my father and smiled. I saw him staring at me really hard through my peripheral vision. My father knew me like a book so he knew something was wrong. But that didn't stop me from putting on a cheerful face.

"Well, if you got it then why was your pops talking to the cops?"

"What are you talking about? When?" I said, trying to figure out what he knew.

"Bitch, stop playing with me! I know you and your pops just left the judge's house."

"Oh yeah, you're right. We did just leave there." I replied calmly.

"Bitch shut up and stop acting like shit is cool. You think I don't know whatcha' doing?"

Instead of commenting, I remained quiet. I knew I couldn't break down in front of my father so I figured if I stayed silent I'd be okay. Otherwise my father would jump in my conversation and start asking me a whole lot of questions.

Unfortunately Kendrick wasn't at all happy about me ignoring him. He snapped. "Why you ain't got shit to say now? Whatcha' trying to keep your pops from finding out that the nigga who killed his friends is on the other end talking to his fucking daughter?"

"No that's not even it. I'm just letting you say whatever it is that you've got to say." I replied even more calmly.

"You know what? You're pissing me off with this bullshit ass calm game you're playing." He chuckled in a menacing way.

"Trust me, it's not like that at all." I told him. My stomach was turning in fucking knots. It felt like I was going to vomit in my mouth at any given moment.

"Listen to me and listen to me good," he said and paused.

"Okay," I said.

"I've got eyes on you and your pops. So, I know your pops was just talking to the cops outside that dead bitch's house. But if I find out that you and your pops are running your mouth about me, I'ma kill him first and then I'm gonna come for you."

After hearing Kendrick mention the word kill in the same sentence with me and my father's name I almost lost it. My head rocked back and forth like I was about to faint. And then I lost all the feeling in my hands so I dropped my cell phone onto the floor of the car. Luckily my father was there to gain control of the steering. "Baby, are you alright? Pull over." He yelled.

I can't say how it happened, but my father helped me navigate my car over to the side of the road. And after he helped me park my car, he placed the back of his right hand against my forehead. "What's wrong baby? Are you sick?" he wanted to know.

I laid my head back against the headrest to calm myself down and gather my thoughts. "Are you feeling hot or something?" his questions continued.

"No, I'm fine." I finally said.

"No you are not." He spat and then he climbed out of the passenger seat. I watched him walk around the front of the car and when he reached the driver side door, he demanded that I get out so he could drive. Without giving him any lip, I climbed out of the car and allowed him to drive my car.

As soon as he drove back onto the open road, he went straight into question mode. "Who the hell were you just talking to that got you all bent out of shape like this? They could've caused you to get into a major car accident." My father hissed.

"Daddy it was nobody." I said, refusing to divulge who I was talking to or what we were talking about.

"The devil is a liar. No don't start that lying stuff Kira. You know I can smell one from a mile away."

"Daddy, it's nothing that I can't handle." I replied with confidence.

"Are you and Dylan having problems? Was that him screaming at you?" My father asked. It was obvious that he was not going to let this issue go away.

"No daddy, Dylan and I aren't having problems. And no that was not him on the phone."

"Don't lie to me Kira. You know I don't like liars."

"Daddy, I'm not lying." I whined because he was starting to get on my nerves. It was bad enough that I had to carry the burden of keeping us both alive on my shoulders, so why ride me?

By the time we had arrived to the valet area of my apartment building my father had talked my head off. He wouldn't let up about the phone conversation I had just had. In his head I wouldn't be talking to any other guy and allow them to get me upset to the point that I'd lose control of my car. Too bad I can't tell him the real reason behind my sudden mental breakdown. I guess I'm going to have to ride this ride alone.

Bull Shit Artist

D ylan wasn't at the apartment when my father and I walked through the front door. I dropped my keys down on the table in the foyer and headed towards the kitchen to get an aspirin and a bottle of water. "Want something to drink?" I asked my father after he entered into the kitchen.

"Do you have tea?" he asked as he took a seat on one of the barstools at the bar area of my kitchen.

"Of course, what kind would you like?"

"Surprise me." He said.

While I prepared a cup of hot tea for my father, he started talking about Mr. and Mrs. Mahoney's murders and what type of people they were. I dreaded hearing about them, because of the guilt that came with it. But in this very moment I didn't have a choice, especially with the fact that my father needed someone to talk to. So, how can I tell him to shut his mouth? Believe me, it wouldn't end well.

"You know the detective said that as soon as they finish working on their leads that he was going to call me and give me an update." He started off saying.

"That's good daddy." I said, with little enthusiasm. My heart was beating at the speed of a fucking Porsche. I figured that if they had evidence that would implicate Kendrick or one of his henchmen then my name would surely come up. I can't let that happen. I'm not built for prison life. No way, fuck that! "You know the Mahoney's neighbors said that they believed that Mr. Mahoney was involved in the drug game." I blurted out.

"That's a fucking lie. Where did they get that ridiculous information from?" he roared.

He was seething at the mouth. The idea that the neighbors had something bad to say about Mr. Mahoney offended him. But he'll get over it whether he liked it or not.

"Daddy, I know Mr. Mahoney was a good friend and colleague, but those people I was talking to where his neighbors, so they got a chance to see him away from work. Now do you think that they would make up something like that?" I tried to reason with him. Well I was really trying to shift the guilt I was feeling, because of my involvement in their murders. Besides that, I knew my father was going to stop at nothing until he helped the cops solve the murders so I figured that if I threw in a couple of monkey wrenches and some fictitious information then I would be successful in sabotaging their investigation.

"Kira, please don't insult me or my friends." He replied sarcastically.

"Daddy, I'm not trying to insult you or your friends. I'm only telling you what those people said." I said apologetically.

"So, did they tell you that Mr. Mahoney came back from the dead and murdered his wife?" he continued talking sarcastically.

I sat my father's tea down on the bar. "No daddy, they didn't." I said calmly.

"Well, what other garbage did they have to say?" he continued to probe me for more answers. His eyes were blood shot red like he was on the verge of crying. So, I did everything in my power to back out of the conversation.

"Daddy, let's leave this whole thing alone. You're sitting here like you are about to cry. And it will hurt me to my heart if I see that." I said, trying to reason with him.

"I'm not about to cry. My eyes are red because I wanna rip somebody's head off their shoulders. So If I had the chance to see the person that's behind the Mahoney murders, I would have my way with him." He explained.

I could see the hurt in my father's face. And I didn't know how long I was going to be able to keep this secret from him. I just hoped and prayed that after this mess blows over I could go back to my normal life without looking over my shoulders.

Ten minutes passed and Dylan walked into the apartment. He walked in the kitchen with a big smile and greeted my father with a handshake. "How are you Mr. Wade? It's nice to see you." He said.

After they shook hands, my father came out of left field and asked Dylan about our relationship. "Were you on the phone yelling at Kira an hour or so ago?"

Dylan looked at me and then he looked back at my father. "You mean an hour or so today?" Dylan asked.

"Daddy, I already told you that that was not Dylan who I was talking to on the phone." I interjected.

"Well, who was it?" My father pressed the issue.

"Yeah, who was it?" Dylan wanted to know.

With both men confronting me with information concerning my phone conversation with Kendrick, it felt like I was being tag teamed. And that was not a good feeling so I came back swinging, metaphorically that is. "It was my boss at the dealership okay." I yelled. I figured that if I yelled and showed some emotions that I would come across like I was finally telling the truth.

"Well, why didn't you say that in the first place?" My father asked.

"Never mind why she didn't tell you that Mr. Wade I wanna know why he was he screaming on you?" Dylan questioned me.

"Dylan, it wasn't nothing really."

"It had to be something for him to call you this time of the night." Dylan shot back.

"Look you two, the reason why my boss called me with an attitude was because I allowed a customer of mine to take one of the dealerships' cars without properly filling out the appropriate paperwork. That's it. Now are y'all satisfied?" I said, hoping my lie would be sufficient enough for them to leave me alone. Right now I needed some rest and that was what I intended to do. "I'm out of here." I told them both and threw up my deuces as I exited the kitchen.

After I left the kitchen my father started talking Dylan's head off about the Mahoney murders. My bedroom wasn't that far away from the kitchen so I could hear every word they uttered from their mouths. "So, how are you feeling right now?" Dylan asked him.

"Well, it's kind of hard to put into words, especially when you have two people that you really love get taken away from you so sudden. They were some good people. And they didn't deserve to die like they did." My father explained.

"Yeah, I saw you on TV with your friend's wife so to hear that she got killed right after that was crazy."

"Yes it was. She was the pillar of our community. She organized a lot of charity functions so she could donate funds to the homeless shelters in the area. And she had a non-profit organization for battered women. Now please explain to me why some heartless bastard would want to harm her?"

"I wished I had the answer to that question Mr. Wade." I heard Dylan say. But Dylan was lying. He knew why the Mahoney's were killed because the streets were talking.

So, has the cops said anything to you about maybe having a suspect?" Dylan continued to pry.

"As of right now, no. But one of the detectives assured me that they had some pretty good leads and as soon as things start to come together, then he's gonna bring me up to speed on everything."

"Well, do they know why they were killed?"

"They believe my friend was robbed and ended up getting killed because they didn't want to leave any witnesses. But as far as his wife is concerned, our only guess is that they were tired of her bringing a lot of media attention to the case so they got rid of her."

"Have you spoken with anyone from their family?"

"Yes, I have."

"So, how are they dealing with it?"

"Really hard."

"Have they started with funeral arrangements?"

"Yes. They've just decided to have their funeral together." I heard him say. He and Dylan ended up having almost an hour-long conversation. Knowing how talkative my father was, Dylan cut him off. He did it tactfully of course. And after he gave my father the "*I'm tired and need to get some rest*" spiel, he showed my dad to the guest room and left him there.

Dylan came in our bedroom a couple seconds later. He started taking off his clothes so he could get into bed. "You know you're not sleeping in here tonight." I told him in a whisper.

"Is it because of your dad?" Dylan said as he hovered over the foot of the bed.

"Duh," I replied sarcastically.

"But this is my house." Dylan began to protest.

"It's my house too. So, let's show some respect." I continued to whisper.

He began to pout like a little boy. "You know I am not happy about this." He said.

"Baby stop whining." I brushed him off.

He took a seat on the edge of the bed. "Look, I'll do it tonight. But I'm sleeping in here tomorrow night." He assured me.

The room became really quiet for a minute or so. But then I said, "I heard you in there talking to my dad about the murders."

"Yeah, I only brought it up because he was looking so out of it."

"I can't believe he thinks that his friend was robbed and killed."

"That's only because that's the only side his friend showed him."

"Well, while he was talking to the detective tonight I overheard the Mahoney's neighbors saying that they heard that Mr. Mahoney was dealing drugs. And that his death was probably triggered from a bad drug deal."

"So you're telling me that you went over to those people's crib?"

"He made me take him over there, so I didn't have a choice."

"Yes you did have a choice Kira. Do you have any idea how fucking hot that place is right now?" Dylan snapped. He raised his voice and I knew my father heard him.

"Can you lower your voice please?" I pleaded.

"Fuck that! This is my house. And you are my woman. So, how would I look allowing you to run out there to those people's house with your father like y'all are fucking CSI or something? The niggas that killed those people are always on the prowl looking to eliminate anyone that poses a threat to them. So, if they happen to get word that you and him are trying to help the police lock them up, they're gonna get rid of y'all asses too!" Dylan snapped.

"Don't you think I know all of that?" I replied as I sat up in the bed. I was getting really pissed off with the lack of respect he was displaying knowing that my father was in the next room.

"Well, act like you know it," he came back at me.

Before I could respond, my father knocked on my bedroom door. "Hey you guys, I'm coming in." he said and opened the door.

Luckily I was dressed appropriately, but I knew Dylan was going to say something to me about it later. "Is everything alright?" my dad asked as he peeped his head into our room.

"Yes, everything is fine daddy." I told him.

"Are you sure? Because I could've sworn that I heard you two in here arguing about me."

"Dylan is just concerned about our safety dad, that's all." I tried to explain.

"So, you think I made a bad judgment call by having my daughter take me over to my friend's house so I could talk to the homicide investigators?"

"Listen Mr. Wade, no disrespect but I don't think that was a good idea. I mean, if you want to go out there and talk to the cops all night long then that's on you. But when you involve Kira I can't stand by and allow it to happen."

"Do you realize that we're talking about my daughter?" My father asked sarcastically. I could tell that he was losing his patience very fast.

"Yes sir I do. But she's gonna be my wife soon so I feel it's my duty to lay down some ground rules."

"Oh so you're planning on marrying her, huh?"

"Alright daddy, and Dylan let's drop it. I'm tired and I'm ready to go to bed!" I interjected and slid out of bed. I marched over to my bedroom door, grabbed my father's hand and escorted him back to the guest room. It only took me about five minutes to calm him down. I promised him that I'd talk to

Dylan in his defense since he felt like Dylan disrespected him.

By the time I went back to my bedroom I noticed that Dylan had already left. I was so happy because I was tired and after everything that happened today, I needed to catch myself some ZZZZZ's.

Taking Sides

The following morning Dylan got up and left the apartment before my father and I had awakened. So, while I was in the kitchen fixing myself a cup of hot tea my father joined me. "Good morning." He said and took a seat on one of the barstools.

"Good morning to you too." I replied. "Are you in the mood for a cup of hot tea." I asked him.

"Why sure." He told me.

"How did you sleep?" I asked.

"Pretty good considering what I had to go through last night." He said putting emphasis on the last four words.

"Daddy please don't start up this morning. I'm trying to have a positive and productive day."

"And I want you to have that, but I will say that your boyfriend is officially on my shit list. Speaking of which, I heard him when he left out of here bright and early."

"Am I supposed to comment on the fact that he left early this morning?"

"No. You don't have to say a word. But I would like for you to explain why he felt like he had the authority to challenge me the way he did?"

"Daddy he wasn't challenging you. He was just being a man and voicing his concerns about my safety. Come on, you can't fault him for wanting me to stay out of harms way, especially with all the drama I experienced in my past." I said as I placed his cup of tea in front of him.

"Kira honey, that doesn't excuse his behavior. He needs to learn how to talk to me."

"You two just need to spend more time together. And then maybe it would be less awkward when you come around."

"Things are fine the way they are. But I would like to know what did Dylan mean when he said that the guys that killed the Mahoney's are always on the prowl? Does he know who they are?"

A ball of anxiety crept inside of me and I was about to have a mental breakdown. I couldn't believe he asked me that. And what was I going to tell him? I knew I couldn't tell him the truth because this conversation wouldn't end well. It would literally be a fucking disaster. So, I played it cool and said, "No daddy, he doesn't know who killed the Mahoneys. All he was saying was that the guys that killed Mr. Mahoney had to be on the prowl because they came back and killed his wife, which is why he got upset about me going over there with you."

"Does he realize that I have protected you all your life and I don't plan on stopping?"

"Of course he does. It's just that the streets are more dangerous now than they have ever been. So, he wants me to be a little more cautious when I'm out there."

"I share his sentiments. But I don't need him telling me what's right and what's wrong when it concerns you. I can handle that department."

"Okay daddy, you're right." I said, trying to defuse the conversation. I realized that it didn't matter what I said, he was going to disagree with it. So, I changed the subject. "What do you plan to do today?" I asked him. I wanted some alone time so I hoped he wasn't going to ask me to drive him around.

"I really hadn't thought about it. I do know that I am going to touch basis with the detective. Who knows he may have found a suspect."

"Look daddy, I know Mr. Mahoney and his wife were good friends to you, but I would prefer if you'd just let the cops call you. All of this running around and doing press conferences is just a bit too much."

"So, you're trying to tell me what to do again?"

"No, I'm not. I just want you to be careful. I don't want to get a phone call from that detective telling me that you got killed."

"That's not going to happen. I have a shotgun. Mrs. Mahoney didn't."

"That's not the point dad. Whoever killed those people are insane."

"Baby girl, don't get all worked up. I am going to be fine." He told me and then he took a sip of his tea.

It seemed like every time I tried to dissuade my father from getting in over his head with his friends' murder cases, he dismissed me like I'm a fucking salesperson. Yes, I sale cars now, but I wasn't trying to sale him one. I'm trying to keep his ass alive but he won't listen. So, will he have to come face to face with a gun before he realizes that those people aren't playing? Or am I going to have to tell him everything I know? Either way, something is going to happen, whether I like it or not.

Shit Starter

After the grueling conversation my father and I had he decided that he wanted me to take him home since he needed to shower and change clothes. I was so fucking happy after he got out of my car and went into his house. Talk about drama-free!

Well, being drama-free only lasted for a few minutes because as soon as I got back on the road my cell phone rang. It was Dylan so I answered it. "Hello," I said.

"Where are you?" he wanted to know.

"I just dropped my father off and now I'm on my way back home. Why?"

"I'm at the crib holding another nigga's driver's license." He spat.

Once again, I was hit with another anxiety attack. Why the fuck is everybody coming at me with a bunch of bullshit? First it was Kendrick. Then it was my father. And now it's Dylan. Can I get a break? "Who's driver's license is it?" I asked him, with the intent to stall the conversation. I knew who's driver's license he had. And it just dawned on me that I still had it. But why I had it is going to be very hard to explain, especially since that guy worked for Kendrick and he could very well be one of the ones that killed Mr. and Mrs. Mahoney.

"It's that nigga John Crew. He's one of the niggas that work for Kendrick."

"Oh yeah, I remember now. He came by the dealership a few days ago to test drive a car. But I didn't know that I still had his I.D." I lied. I was putting a lot of effort in my story. And I was hoping that Dylan would go for it.

"I thought that you were only supposed to make a copy of it and give it back."

I caught a sharp pain in my side when he pressed the issue about the driver's license. I knew I had to come back strong or else I was going to be in the doghouse. "Yeah, that's normally what I do but now that I think back, someone was using the Xerox machine at the time and since the guy was pressed for time I decided to put it in my pocket and forgot to give it back to him. Speaking of which, I wonder why he hadn't tried to call me so he could get it back?" I said. I wanted to make this situation sound as innocent as possible.

"Are you sure this nigga wasn't trying to holla at you?" Dylan asked.

I had to admit that Dylan was a bit insecure at times. And he had a lot of reasons to be considering how good I look. But in this case, he had nothing to worry about it. John wasn't really trying to buy a car from me. That motherfucker came to he dealership to put fear in my ass. And guess what? He did it.

"Listen Dylan, every nigga that comes to see me at the dealership only come for one thing and that's to buy a car."

"Not all of them."

"Okay, maybe there's been a few guys that tried to holla at me. But that's it. That guy that forgot to get his driver's license from me never tried to holla at me. All he wanted to do was test drive the new Rolls Royce coupe I showed him."

"Probably the only reason why he didn't holla at you was because Kendrick told him I was your man."

"Yeah, you're probably right." I said. At this moment, I had no other choice but to agree with anything he said. A wise woman never opens her mouth until she is told to.

"Well, I want you to come to the crib and get this shit out of here. Take it back to your job or something."

"A'ight. I'll be there in about twenty minutes."

"Is your father coming back over here?"

"I don't think so."

"Well, you need to find out because I ain't trying to go through that shit I went through last night."

"A'ight," I said and then I disconnected our call.

Not In The Mood

Dylan met me at the front door when I entered into our apartment. He stood in the foyer holding up the guy's I.D. in plain sight. My heart dropped into the pit of my stomach. "You're telling me the truth about this lame ass nigga, right?"

After I closed the front door and locked it, I put on the most sincere expression I could muster up. "Of course I am. I mean, look at him. That joker isn't even my type."

"A'ight. Now I'm gonna let this go. But I better not hear nothing about you and him in the streets."

"Don't worry. You won't." I replied confidently.

"A'ight, well take this shit before I throw it in the trash." He commented and handed me the guy's driver's license.

After I took the I.D. I stuck it inside my Chanel handbag and then I placed the handbag on the small table near the mirror in the foyer. When I walked away from the table Dylan grabbed onto my arm and whirled me around until I fell into his arms. He kissed me on my lips and asked me if he could have five minutes of my time.

"For what?" I asked but I knew what he wanted.

"I wanna give you some of this dick." He said.

"I'm too tired right now. Can we do it later?" I whined. I wasn't in the mood to fuck. Giving him some pussy was the last thing on my mind. What I needed was a vacation away from this place. Hearing about another dead body surfacing would definitely send me over the edge and I may not come back from it this time. I just want everything to go back the way they were.

"Please," he began to beg. He started kissing me on my neck thinking that that shit was going to work, but it wasn't.

"Dylan, I told you I am tired."

"I'll tell you what, I'll do all the work. All you have to do is slide your pants down and bend over." He explained.

"That's still not going to work." I said and broke away from his grip. I wasn't trying to be a bitch. I just wanted to be left alone so I could gather my thoughts and hopefully figure out how I was going to give Kendrick's boy his driver's license back. The thought of seeing him again made my skin crawl. And the fact that he threatened my life gave me a sickening feeling in my stomach. So, I figured if I got one of the receptionists at the dealership to call him then I wouldn't have to worry about any of that happening again.

"So, you're just gonna leave me standing here with a hard on?" he yelled while I walked away.

"You're a big boy. You can handle it." I yelled back.

Give Me Two Reasons

When Dylan realized that he wasn't getting any pussy, he sat around in the living room and watched a couple of episodes of the reality show Pawn Stars. I on the other hand called the dealership and got my girl Nancy Cox on the phone. She was one of the three receptionists that worked at the dealership. She was a La La Anthony look-alike but she had a comedic side to her and she was a firecracker when she wanted to be. We clicked on the first day I started working there. She was a few years younger than I was, but she held her own when she and I would occasionally go to happy hour at the exclusive members-only Sky Bar down on the strip. "Hey Nancy, what's up?"

"Nothing much, what's up with you?"

"Well, a customer of mine forgot to get his driver's license back from me the other day, so would you call him and let him know that we have it and that he can come by the dealership to pick it up."

"Where is it?"

"I've got it. But I'm getting ready to leave my apartment so I can drop it off to you. I should be there in about fifteen minutes."

"Okay. What's his name and his phone number?"

"Wait a minute, let me get it out of my phone." I said and then I paused for a moment. "His number is 555-1004. And his name is John Crew." I continued.

"Alright, I got it. So, you want me to call him now?"

"Yes. Call him now." I instructed her.

"Okay. Well, I guess I'll see you when you get here."

"Yep, so I'll see you then." I assured her and then I disconnected our call.

On my way back out of the apartment, Dylan made a beeline to the door and stood there with his car keys in hand. "Ready?" he said.

"Yeah, I'm ready but where are you going?" I questioned him.

"I'm going with you."

"And when did you decide this?"

"Do you think I'm going to let you leave this house today without me, especially with all the dumb shit that's going on with your dad and those people that got killed?"

"So, what are you now, my bodyguard?"

"I'll be whatever you want me to be. So let's go." He replied and escorted me out the apartment.

Dylan had two cars. The first one was a white, 2014 Range Rover – HSE and the second one was a black, 2012 Porsche Panamera. Today he decided to cruise around Miami in the Porsche. A minute and a half into the drive Dylan got a phone call from his sister Sonya. His cell phone was synced to his car so the call was automatically connected to the speaker-phone, which allowed me to hear the entire call. "What's up sis?"

"Dylan I think Bruce put his hands on mama again." She said.

"Why you say that?" his tone changed.

"Because she has a few scratches on her face. She's trying to make me believe that the scratches came from her dog."

"Where is Bruce?"

"I'm not sure. But I know he's not here."

"I gotta' take Kira up to the dealership for a second and then we're gonna come over there. So, give me about thirty minutes."

"Okay." She said.

As soon as Dylan hung up with his sister Sonya he gave me this sinister look and I knew that it wouldn't go away until he was face to face with his mother's new husband Bruce. "Kira, I swear on everything I love that I am going to kill that nigga today." He roared.

"Stop it. Don't talk like that." I told him, hoping that I'd calm him down.

"I'm sorry but I can't. Do you know how bad it hurts me to hear about that nigga putting his hands on my mama? I can't stand around and let him treat her like she's his fucking punching bag. I mean, I've already warned this nigga one time. So, do you think I'm gonna let this shit slide"

"Dylan, I'm not saying that."

"Then what are you saying?" he replied sarcastically.

"All I'm saying is go over there and check everything out. If you see that your mother has been hit on, do what you gotta do. But please don't kill him. I need you out here on the streets. Not in jail." I told him.

"Fuck that! If I see one scratch on my mother I'm going to jail. Just call my attorney and tell him to be ready to come and bail me out."

"Yeah, alright." I said. I figured since he had already made up his mind that he was going to kill his mother's husband, I just stepped back and allowed him to have the floor. I had too much shit going on in my own life to be worried about Bruce's life. From where I stood, he had a death wish. Dylan had already warned him before, so I'm going to stay in my lane and keep it moving.

When Dylan pulled into the parking lot of the dealership, I stepped out of the car and headed inside the building with John's drivers license in hand. Nancy was sitting at the front desk when I approached her. She smiled and greeted me. "You're looking pretty rested." She commented.

"That's what happens when you take a few days off." I replied and then I handed her the driver's license.

She took a long look at it. "He's kind of cute."

"Don't even go there. I promise you he's not worth your time." I warned her.

"What do you mean? He looks like he's cool and laid back."

"Well, he's not the cool and laid back guy you think he is."

"So, he's a bad boy, huh?"

"He's worse than that. Now stick the license in your drawer until he comes by to get it." I instructed her.

"Okay. Calm down. I get the picture." She commented and then she shoved the I.D. into the top drawer.

"Has it been busy today?" I changed the subject.

"Sort of. Oh yeah, speaking of which, you've had a couple of customers come by looking for you. They said they tried calling your cell phone, but they're always getting your voicemail. And for the ones who tried leaving messages said that your mailbox is full. So, do everyone a favor and start answering your phone or at least clear out your voicemail messages."

"Sure. I can do that."

"So, what are you getting ready to do now?" Nancy wanted to know.

"Well, Dylan and I are going over to his mother's house to visit and then we'll probably get something to eat after that."

"Have fun."

"I don't know how much fun I will have. But I will try."

Beat You Like You Stole Something

I started to stay in the car while Dylan went inside his mother's home, but after I saw Sonya's face when she came to the front door to let Dylan in, I knew it would be a good idea that I accompany him before it became a blood bath in there. "Hold the door, I'm coming." I yelled after I got out of the car.

Sonya held the door open for me as I approached the house. She gave me a half smile. I smiled back. "Thank you," I said as I walked by her.

"No problem." She replied and then she closed the front door.

"Where is everyone?" I asked.

"In the family room. And Bruce is here too." She said.

"Really!?" I replied and then I proceeded down the hall. My heart started beating rapidly. I braced myself for what I was about to walk into.

As soon as I turned the corner and entered into the family room I saw Mrs. Daisy first so I zoomed in on the scratches she had near her noise and cheek area of her face. She was sitting on the lounge chair next to Bruce trying to explain how she got the scratches. Mrs. Daisy was a brown-skin, medium build woman. She reminded me of Gladys Knight. She was such a sweet lady, which was why I couldn't see why her new husband Bruce would put his hands on her.

With bloodshot red eyes, Bruce sat next to Mrs. Daisy like a pup with his tail between his legs, the total opposite of what he really looked like. Bruce was a dark skin, big guy. He had to be 5'11, and weighed at least 230lbs. So, why act like a little pussy when your wife's son comes to her rescue? Whatever he had on his mind will be revealed at any second. "Mama, stop taking up for this nigga." Dylan barked.

His sister Sonya took a seat on the sofa across from her mother and Bruce. "Yeah, mama, there's no way you got those scratches on your face from the dog." Sonya added. She was definitely adding fuel to the fire.

"Nigga why you keep putting your hands on my mama? Didn't I tell you that if you did it again I was going to kill you?" Dylan roared, literally spitting in his face with every word he uttered. He stood over top of Bruce like he was chastising him.

Bruce nodded his head.

"Well if I told you that then why does she have scratches all over her face?" Dylan continued to interrogate him.

"I told you he didn't do this!" Mrs. Daisy yelled at Dylan. But Dylan totally ignored her.

"Answer me Bruce! Answer me now!" Dylan snapped.

"Listen to your mama. She already said I didn't hit her." He finally said, but his words were barely audible.

Without any warning Dylan lunged back and plunged a heavy blow to Bruce's right eye. Bruce fell back on the sofa helpless. That didn't deter Dylan from hitting him a few more times. WACK! WACK! WACK! "I told you not to put your hands on my mama again didn't I?" Dylan snapped.

"Stop it Dylan. Leave him alone." Mrs. Daisy cried out. I saw how badly it affected her to see her son beat up on her man. And now that I looked closely at how badly Dylan was hurting this guy, it kind of affected me too. So when Mrs. Daisy stood up from the sofa and tried to stop Dylan from hitting Bruce, I got up and ran over to help her. Sonya only sat back and watched everything play out.

"Dylan, please stop hitting him. You're gonna kill him!" Mrs. Daisy screamed.

"Yes baby, that's enough. Please stop. Look at his face, blood is everywhere." I interjected.

"Nah, fuck that! I'm gonna kill this nigga today." Dylan yelled then he hit Bruce two more times.

"I'm calling the police!" Mrs. Daisy screamed. And scrambled away from the sofa where Dylan had Bruce penned down. Luckily Sonya grabbed Mrs. Daisy's cell phone away from her before she was able to dial 911.

"No mama, I can't let you call the police on Dylan." I heard Sonya say.

"Give me my phone!" Mrs. Daisy screamed. She was now sobbing uncontrollably. And I was starting to feel sorry for her and Bruce. It was so much commotion going on in this house it felt like I was about to have a mental breakdown. I wanted this mess to stop so I pleaded with Dylan to stop hitting Bruce. "Baby, you gotta stop before you kill him." I begged as I tugged him by his waist. Finally he stopped hitting Bruce. But when he stood up, he had plenty of Bruce's blood on his hands and shirt. And Bruce was barely recognizable. Every inch of his face was swollen. I could hardly see his eyeballs. He was in bad shape.

"Get out of my house!" Mrs. Daisy screamed at Dylan. "You too Sonya. Get out of my house now!" she continued.

I thought Dylan would've tried to calm his mother down and apologize for the mess he made, but he didn't. So while he grabbed a handful of paper towels from the kitchen, I whispered an apology to her and then I followed Dylan and Sonya out of the house.

Dylan and Sonya said a few words to each other and then we all drove away from the house. "What do you think is going to happen now?" I asked him while I watched him wipe the blood away from his hands.

"You mean with Bruce and my moms?"

"Well, yeah..."

"At this point I could care less just as long as he keeps his hands to himself."

"Do you think they'll call the police?"

"I can't think about that now."

"Well, at some point you're gonna have to Dylan. Now I know you love your mother and I know you'll die first before you let someone hurt her, but you just beat up her husband. And she wasn't at all happy about it. So, if you plan on being in her life, you're gonna have to make a few adjustments as far as how you handle things dealing with her and Bruce."

"Fuck that! I'm not doing shit! I would be less than a man if I sit around and act like it's okay for him to put his hands on my mother. My daddy would turn over in his grave if I let that shit ride."

"Dylan I'm not saying that. What I am saying is, there's a way to handle things like that. And considering what you do for a living, I would hate for you to get some unnecessary heat on you. That's all." I explained.

"Well, I appreciate your concern. But I got this." He assured me and then he turned his attention to the passenger side window. I saw him gazing at everything from people to the buildings, which was a huge indication that he was in deep thought.

Dylan and I drove back to our apartment in silence. The only time he talked was when he got on his cellphone and called his partner Nick. They didn't talk much. Dylan spoke briefly about the ass beating he gave his mother's husband. Then they said a few codes and before Dylan disconnected their call, I heard him tell Nick to come by our apartment within the next hour. Nick said a few more words and that was the end of that.

When we pulled up in front of our building, Dylan took off his shirt and wrapped it around his right hand. After we got out of the car, we rushed onto the elevator avoiding all the residents we knew. We weren't in the mood to do a lot of explaining about Dylan's cuts and bruises. Telling one lie would roll into another lie. That was a bullet we both wanted to dodge. Thankfully we arrived at our apartment without any interruptions. What a day's work that was!

Who Calls The Shots?

After the firestorm at Dylan's mother's house, Dylan took a long hot bath. And when he was done, I pulled out the first aid kit and I put a number of bandages on both of his hands. He looked like Money Mayweather when I was done with him. "Alright champ! Don't hurt nobody!" I teased to lighten up the mood a little.

He smiled back and kissed me on the lips. "Now that's gonna cost you." I clowned around.

"You saw how I laid that nigga out behind my mother? Let me find out somebody fucking with you and watch what I do to them." he said in a jokingly manner but I know he was dead serious.

"Oh hush." I smiled. "So, what are we going to eat?" I asked.

"Let's order a pizza." He suggested.

"Oh yeah, that sounds good." I replied.

"Call the spot between 1st and 2nd called Big Pink."

"Got them on speed dial." I told him.

It didn't take me long to get the people at Big Pink on the phone and place my order. A couple of minutes after I hung up with them my phone rang. And like clock work, it was my father. One part of me dreaded to answer him. But then I decided against it because he only had me. And if he couldn't get in touch with me then who would he be able to call? "Hey daddy, what's up?" I asked.

"Got some good news." He said, sounding very energetic.

"What is it?"

"I just got off the phone with Detective Grimes and he said that he had some information for me but that he needs me, to come down to the station."

"That's it?" I said hesitantly.

"What do you mean is that it?"

"He's got some information for you but you got-ta' go down to the police station to get it. What kind of mess is that?" I spat. I was getting really irritated with this whole thing. Why couldn't my father just leave this whole case alone? Does he not see that he's digging himself a hole that he may not be able to get out? I wished that he would open his fucking eyes.

"Kira, I don't need the negativity honey. I only called you because I wanted you to take me down there."

"I'm sorry daddy, but I am not going down to no-body's police station. And you shouldn't either. Let those detectives do their job and stay out of it." I warned him.

"Listen to me little girl, I am going down there whether you take me or not."

"Well you know what daddy? Then go on down there."

"Oh don't worry. I will. And I'll talk to you later."

"Okay daddy." I said and then I heard the line click. I knew our conversation was over but I didn't want to let the phone go.

"Is he gone?" Dylan whispered.

"Yeah, he's gone." I said and that's when I laid the phone down on the sofa next to us.

"Did he just say that he was on his way down to the police station?"

"Yep, he sure did."

"What the fuck is wrong with that guy?"

"I don't know."

"So, he hasn't listened to anything you told him, huh?"

"Seems that way."

"Well, you know it's out of your hands right?"

I hesitated for a second and then I said, "I guess so."

"And do you realize that you may not be able to be seen with him?"

"Wait a minute Dylan, I just can't turn my back on my father cold turkey." I protested.

"But if he continues to fuck with the cops and those niggas find out about it, they're gonna come after him. And it ain't gonna matter who's with him because those niggas will take that person's life too."

"There's gotta' be another way around this." I said aloud, trying to spin this situation around to avoid telling Dylan that Kendrick already knew who my father was. Not to mention that he has already given my father and I death threats. Pretending to be naïve about this whole thing was becoming unbearable. Something has to change.

I sat there on the sofa next to Dylan as he ran down different scenarios that could happen if my father continued to stick his nose where it didn't belong, all of which I didn't want to hear. "Do you think I wanna keep hearing you tell me what those niggas would do to my father if they found out he was helping the police?"

"It's better to hear it from me than somebody else."

"But you're acting like I'm new to the street life. I know what time it is."

"Well act like you do. And shut that shit down with your father and the police before you have to plan his funeral."

I sucked my teeth and stood up to my feet. "I am so over all this bullshit!" I said and then I stormed off.

Why Be Fooled?

When the food finally came I couldn't eat one bite of it. I couldn't get my mind off my father hanging down at the police station talking to the detectives. The fact that Kendrick knew that my father and I were at the Mahoney's house talking to the cops the night Mrs. Mahoney was killed made me question the fact that they were probably watching me and my father's every move. If that was indeed the case, then my dad and I were up shits creek without a paddle.

I had no idea how I was going to cope with my father being out there on the streets alone. But I couldn't run out of the house for the fear that that may cause Dylan to jump down my throat. Thankfully his business partner Nick stopped by the house to check on Dylan. This moment couldn't have come at a better time. We needed as much distraction as we could possibly get considering all the shit that I was dealing with my father and the murders.

After Nick yelled hello to me, he and Dylan retreated to the living room. "Kira, got you wrapped up pretty good I see." Nick joked. "You look like you're about to get in the ring."

I heard Dylan laugh at Nick's joke and then things got serious. "How are the numbers looking?" Dylan asked.

"Everything is moving steady. And it looks like we're gonna have to re-up by the end of the week." Nick said. Nick had a unique way in which he talked. He sounded like he was from Cuba or the Dominican Republic, but from what Dylan says, Nick was born and raised here in Miami. In addition to his sexy voice, Nick was also handsome. His hair was black with big locks of curls and his face was so smooth I'm sure it felt like a newborn baby's ass. He definitely resembled the Latin singer Ricky Martin, but better.

"Are we going back to our same source?" Dylan asked.

"I was hoping that you'd sample some of Luis' work, since he was going to give us a good deal. And who knows, his shit maybe better."

"Let's do that then. Call him and set it up."

"Are you going to join us?"

"Of course I will."

"Alright. Well, I guess our meeting is adjourned." Nick said.

Once Nick and Dylan settled things concerning their dope houses and the correct accounting of the revenue that came from them, Nick yelled goodbye to me and made his exit.

Not to long after Nick left the apartment Dylan came back into our bedroom carrying a Bloomingdale's bag. In the bag was a shoebox filled with money. I watched Dylan as he filled up the safe with the money. "I'm putting eighty grand in the stash." He said.

"Okay." I replied. Keeping count was my other job. Every time Dylan put money away, he always gave me the figures so I could keep the numbers straight. Nick thinks that he is Dylan's right hand, but in actuality, I'm his right hand. And that's the way Dylan and I intended to keep it.

Survival of the Fittest

The very next day I got a few calls from my father, which of course I ignored because Dylan was around. Then about thirty minutes later I got a call from Jason wanting to know when I was coming back into work. Everyone including him was under the impression that I took leave from work because I was having some family issues. "I've had a lot of your personal customers calling and coming by wanting to know when you're coming back to work." he said.

"Did you tell them that I was dealing with a family emergency?" I asked.

"Yes, I did. But they weren't trying to hear anything I had to say. As a matter of fact, one of your clients named Carlos told me to tell you that he will only spend his money with you and that he'd be back in a couple of days. So, Kira, please say that you'll come back for a couple of hours to handle that deal and then you can go back on leave."

"I don't know Jason. I mean, I'm not in the best spirits right now." I said.

"Okay, I'll tell you what. I'll give you an extra five percent on the deal." He bargained.

I pondered over Jason's offer for a moment and then I said, "Okay, have Nancy call him and tell him that I have a 12pm appointment available for today."

"Will do. See you in an hour." Jason replied.

I jumped to my feet after I hung up with Jason. I hopped in the shower for about fifteen minutes, and once I was done bathing, I combed my hair back into a ponytail I slipped on a cute, blue, Oscar de la renta pencil skirt, a beautiful floral, sheer blouse by Burberry, and to bring my whole ensemble together I slipped on a pair of four and half inch black Giuseppe Zanotti pumps. I looked like a million bucks.

"I've got a 12 o'clock appointment at the dealership so I'll see you when I get back." I told Dylan, who by this time was in his closet looking for something to wear.

"Nick is coming by here to pick me up so I probably won't be here when you get back."

"Okay. Well, call me later if you need anything." I told him and then I left the apartment.

"A'ight," he replied.

Nancy greeted me with a warm smile when I walked through the front doors of the dealership. "You're back."

"Just for today." I said as I approached the front desk.

"Guess what?" she whispered.

I leaned on the front desk to get closer to her. "What?" I whispered back.

"Remember when you gave me the driver's license to give to that guy?"

"Yeah, what happened?"

"Well when he stopped by to pick up his license he asked me if he could take me out to dinner and of course I said yes. So last night he picked me up from my apartment and we went out and had a ball."

My heart dropped after hearing Nancy tell me that she went out with that crazy ass nigga John. "What made you go out with him? Do you know what he does for a living?"

Nancy smiled with excitement. "The way he treated me last night, he could be a mass murderer and I wouldn't care."

"You fucked him didn't you?"

Nancy smiled bashfully. "Yes, I did and it was the best sex I had in a long time."

"Well guess what?"

"What?"

"You fucked a mass murderer!"

Nancy giggled. "Stop playing. I know you're joking." She commented.

"No I am not joking. That guy works for one of the most notorious assholes in the city. And I don't think it will be wise for you to hang out with him anymore."

"Well how can I do that when I agreed to go out

with him on a second date tonight?"

"Nancy, I want you to get on the phone right now and cancel your date with him. If you don't you're gonna regret it big time." I warned her.

"But he has already made reservations at the restaurant called Prime 112. I can't cancel on him now. That wouldn't be right."

"Do you want to die?"

"What kind of question is that? Of course not." She replied sadly.

"Well call him and tell him that you can no longer see him again."

Nancy sighed heavily and said, "Alright."

I watched her as she picked up the phone from the front desk. I knew she needed her privacy so I walked away so she could handle her business and get rid of that nigga.

Back in my office, Jason stopped by and thanked me for coming in. "I am truly grateful that you were able to come in." he smiled as he rubbed both of his hands together. All he was thinking about was the money he was going to make from this huge ass sale I was about to bring to his company.

"Jason I didn't do it for the money. I did it for you." I told him.

"Oh wow! That's news to my ears. Thank you." He smiled.

"Just know that as soon as I finish this deal I'm going back home."

"I know. I know. So, I wanna thank you again."

He said and backed his way out of my office.

I smiled. "No problem Jason."

Keep Your Fucking Mouth Shut

Processing the paperwork for Mr. Carlos only took me a little over an hour. He drove off the lot with a late model Bugatti Veyron so Jason was a happy camper. We were all happy campers around there, well almost everyone. On my way out of the building I winked my eye at Nancy and said, "You took care of that, right?"

"Yes, I took care of it." She replied with little to no enthusiasm.

"Trust me, you'll thank me later." I told her as I passed her.

"Kira wait," she said.

I stopped in my tracks. "Yeah, what is it?"

"There's a Detective Grimes waiting in the waiting room to talk to you." She told me.

Totally caught off guard, my mood shifted from excitement to worry. And when I turned around towards the waiting room the detective stood up from his chair and started walking towards me. Pissed off by his unexpected visit I looked at Nancy and said, "How long has he been here?"

"He just got here about three minutes ago. I called your extension but I see why you didn't hear it because you were on your way up here."

"Hi Kira, how are you?" he asked and extended his hand for me to shake. I shook his hand and asked him how could I help him.

"I just need to ask you a few questions."

"Are you rolling solo today?" I asked because his partner was nowhere in sight.

"Detective Lowes had a last minute appointment, so yes, it's just me." He explained. "Is there some-place we can go?" he continued.

"Well, I was on my way to my car. So, I guess you can follow me and ask me whatever it is that you want to."

"Okay, sure. Let's do that." He said.

After I had given the detective the green light to ask me a few questions, he grabbed ahold of the door so I could walk through it and then he escorted me to my car. "You know your father and I keep in close contact with one another right?" he started off as he pulled a small note pad and pen from the inside of his jacket pocket.

"Yes," I said.

"And do you also know that he's been totally co-operative in the investigation involving his friend and just recently his friend's wife?"

"Yes,"

"Okay well, the reason why I came down here is because yesterday your father came down to the station and provided my team with some valuable information that has brought us closer to finding our suspect or suspects. Now part of that information your father shared was about a conversation you had with the Mahoney's neighbors."

I chuckled in a sarcastic manner. "Oh really?" I said and rolled my eyes.

"Is that true?"

"Yeah, I talked to a couple of the neighbors but they did almost all the talking."

"Can you tell me what they were talking about?"

"I really don't remember. I mean, they were saying that they heard Mr. Mahoney was doing business with drug dealers. And that he was probably murdered because of a bad deal."

"Do you remember the name of the neighbor that made that comment?" he asked while he was scribbling something on the note pad.

"No."

"Was it a woman or a man?"

"Woman."

"Do you remember how she looked?"

"It was dark. So, no."

"Do you remember anything else that was said?"

"No. Not that I can recall." I said nonchalantly. At this point in the conversation I was ready to get in my car and go home.

The detective reached in his jacket pocket and handed me his card. "If you remember anything else please call me. It would mean the world to your father if we find the killers."

Irritated to the core I gave the detective the evil eye. "Wait, my father told me that you guys already had a suspect."

"We did. But after his alibi was checked out we had to let him go."

"Who was this suspect?" I asked. I was very curious to know who this person was.

"That I can't tell you."

"So, I can tell you stuff but you can't tell me anything? What kind of B.S. is that?"

"Until this investigation is over and we have the perpetrator in custody I cannot give you any information."

"Oh how freaking convenient! You can have my father running around here doing your job like he's Batman, but I bet if he asked you where you are in the case, you'd give him the cold shoulder just like you're giving me."

"Kira, I'm sorry you feel that way."

"Look man, just take care of my father. Better yet, why don't you tell him that he's treading on dangerous grounds and that he needs to step back so you guys can do your own jobs, because he won't listen to me."

"My colleagues and I have already told him that."

"Well, stop answering his calls. I'm sure he'll get tired of leaving you voicemail messages."

"We can't stop him from calling the station."

"Well, you better do something because if anything happens to him I am going to sue the hell out of the police department." I spat and then I got in my car and pulled off.

Niggas & Their Baggage

I was boiling on the inside after I had that chat with the Detective Grimes. I was pissed off at the fact that he would come to my job unannounced. And then to question me about the shit my father the told him made me even more irritated. More importantly, I wasn't about to stand there and let him squeeze me for information. That wasn't how I was built.

Halfway into my drive I tried to call my father from my cell phone but for some reason the call wouldn't go through. I couldn't get a signal for the life of me. So, I threw my phone down on the passenger seat, put my car on full throttle and sped in the direction of his house.

During the entire drive I constantly looked through the rearview mirror and over my shoulders just to make sure I wasn't being followed. I didn't look over my shoulders this much when I would tag along with Dylan when he picked up money from his spots. What kind of life was I living? Had I ventured into the same lifestyle I had in the past? I would definitely find out sooner than later.

My father's car was parked in his usual place in the driveway. But when I got out of the car and rang the doorbell I didn't see any sign of him. I had a set of keys to his house but I was too afraid to let myself in, especially with everything that has transpired in the last ten days. So once again I started knocking and ringing the doorbell. "Daddy, are you home?" I yelled. "Daddy it's me Kira. Open the door." I yelled once again.

But to no avail my knocks went unanswered. Anxiety crept inside of me and filled my entire body up with a scary feeling that something was wrong. I even started visualizing my father lying down on the floor somewhere in the house dead. Then I thought of the possibility that Kendrick had one of his boys come by here and kidnap him. And now he's being tortured like a fucking pitbull in a dogfight. Either way I looked at it, my father was in a bad situation.

I couldn't stand on the porch anymore after having those bad thoughts running around in my head so I ran back to my car. When I opened the door to get inside my car I heard a voice call my name. "Kira."

When I looked up and saw my father standing at the door I became elated. Harboring the feelings of the cop showing up at my place of employment went straight out of the window. I raced back on the front porch with open arms. "Thank God!" I said and sighed.

"What's wrong? Are you okay?" he asked.

"I've been ringing your doorbell and knocking on the door for at least five minutes, and when you didn't come I thought something happened to you."

"But you have a key. So, why didn't you use it?"

"I don't know." I lied. I refused to tell him the truth. I just couldn't bring myself to do it.

"Come on in." he said. He grabbed my hand and escorted me into the house. We went into the kitchen first. He tried to get me to drink a glass of red wine but I wasn't up for it. He poured himself one instead and then he retreated to the family room. "You know I've been calling you right?"

"Yes daddy, I know. I've been really busy. But I was going to call you back."

"So, what brings you by?"

"Detective Grimes showed up at my job today asking me a bunch of questions and I didn't appreciate it."

"What did he say?"

"Look daddy, I'm not here to go back and forth with you about what he said. But I did come here to tell you to tell your cop friend not to show up at my job again or else I'm going to get him for harassment."

"If you would've answered my phone calls he would not have showed up at your place of business. I called you to go down to the police station with me and you declined to go so how else was the detective going to talk to you?"

"Don't you get it dad? I didn't go to the police station with you because I didn't have anything to say to him or anyone else for that matter."

"Kira, he only wanted you to reiterate what you heard the neighbors say the other night."

"Don't you think I know that now?" I spat.

"Listen baby girl, I don't want to fight you on this. I understand that you don't want to talk to the detective anymore so I respect that. And you will never have to worry about him popping up on you again."

"Thank you." I said. And then I smiled.

It felt good to finally get my father on the same page with me. Now all I had to do was get him to agree that he'd step back and let the cops do their own job. I knew it was a long shot but I went for it anyway. "Think you can step back a few feet and let the cops do their investigation?" I asked.

"Sweetheart I want to tell you yes, but in my heart I can't step back and not do anything. The Mahoney's were my friends."

"Would you stop if your life was in jeopardy?"

"That all depends."

"Depends on what daddy?"

"Is my life in jeopardy?" he asked me. He looked me straight in the eyes like he could see through me. I didn't know whether to lie or tell him the truth.

"I can't answer that. But it wouldn't surprise me considering that Mrs. Mahoney got killed right after she did that press conference."

My father chuckled. "I'll tell you what, if I'm next on the killer's list then so be it. I am a retired Circuit Court Judge so I will not allow anyone to stop me from doing what is right."

I let out a long sigh. "Alright, daddy." I said and threw my hands up.

Right when I was leaving his house he asked me if I'd go with him to Mr. and Mrs. Mahoney's funeral the next day. I reluctantly agreed to go. Immediately thereafter he gave me a time to be ready and said that he'd come by my place to pick me up. I said okay and then we ended the night.

Reckless Ass Bitches

Dylan wasn't supportive of me attending the Mahoney's funeral but because I had promised my father that I would go, there was nothing Dylan could do that would've made me change my mind. I did however promise Dylan that I'd come straight home afterwards.

My father picked me up on time. We went to the church where the funeral was taken place. I couldn't believe that the Mahoney's knew so many people. It was mass hysteria to say the least. There had to be over three hundred people there and half of those people were crying. At one point, I became a little sad. It was definitely an emotional sight to see.

At the end of the funeral service I watched my father pay his respects to a few of the Mahoney's family members and then we left. "That wasn't so bad." I said after we got back into his car.

My father smiled. "I told you it wouldn't be."

"I can't believe that all those people came."

"The Mahoney's were some good people. And that's why I'm doing what's necessary to help bring their killers to justice."

"Daddy please let's not go there again." I commented.

"Okay. Okay. I'm going to let it go." He replied.

"Thank you."

My father drove me back to my apartment and dropped me off. I kissed him on the cheek and asked him what was on his agenda for the rest of the day. "I'm gonna head over to the family's house and mingle with them for a little while."

"Daddy, will you leave those people alone for just one day?"

"Look Kira, I don't tell you what to do so please don't tell me what to do." He replied sarcastically.

Taken aback by his comment, I said, "You know what daddy? You're right. Now you have a nice day."

Before he could make another comment, I closed the passenger side door and stormed away from his car.

Dylan was lying on the sofa when I walked into the house. He smiled as soon as he laid eyes on me. "How was the funeral?" he asked.

"Crowded."

"How did your father act?"

"He didn't break down if that's what you're asking me." I commented while I was taking off my heels. I took a seat next to Dylan and laid my head back against the headrest of the sofa.

"Where is he now?"

"On his way back to the family's house."

"Yo' he better chill out before something happens to his crazy ass." Dylan commented.

"Please don't beat me in the head with another argument about my father." I begged.

"I wasn't going to say anything else."

"Good. Because all I want to do is rest."

"You got it."

1-800-*MISSING*

I hadn't talked to my father since he dropped me off after the funeral, which was two days ago. We left on a bad note so I assumed that he knew I needed some space. I attempted to call him a couple of times but I decided against it. My father has become so wrapped up in the murder investigation involving his friends that he can't think straight, so I figured that it would be best if he did his thing and I did mine.

While I was in the kitchen eating a bowl of cereal my cell phone rang. I looked at the caller I.D. and saw that it was my boss Jason so I answered it. "Please don't call me and tell me that I have another customer there that won't buy a car from anyone else at the dealership." I said.

"No, that's not what I'm calling you for."

"So what's up?"

"Have you talked to Nancy?" he wanted to know.

"Not since the day I came in to help my customer Mr. Carlos. But why you ask?" I asked. I immediately got worried. I hoped nothing bad has happened to her.

"Well, because that was the last day any of us has seen her. We've called her cell phone and it keeps going straight to voicemail. We've called her house but no one is answering the phone there. We've also called her mother and she hasn't seen or talked to her either."

"Wow! That's really strange because Nancy would never not come to work without calling."

"My sentiments exactly." Jason replied.

"Okay. Well, let me make a few calls and I'll call you back if I hear something." I told him.

"Thanks." He said.

I lost my appetite after I got off the phone with Jason. I literally became sick to my stomach at the thought that something bad may have happened to Nancy. I couldn't keep this type of information to myself so I rushed to the bedroom where Dylan was asleep. "Baby, wake up?" I told him.

He was lying on his stomach so after he turned over on his back and adjusted his eyes he asked me what was wrong?

I sat on the bed next to him and said, "I just got a call from my boss Jason asking me if I've heard or seen Nancy because she hasn't been to work in two days."

"Are you talking about that chick that works at the front deck?"

"Yes."

"So why did he call you?"

"Because he knows that she and I have hung out a few times."

"Well, have you talked to her?"

"The last time I saw and talked to her was two days ago when I went to work for a couple of hours to do that Bugatti deal with my customer. And what's so crazy about that was when I stopped at the front desk to talk to her, she started smiling and telling me about the day before when she called John to come and pick up his driver's license and when he got there they started talking and hit it off. Then she says that she had so much fun with him that she agreed to go out on another date. So, I immediately told her to call him and cancel the date because he wasn't the type of guy she needed to be dealing with. So, she got a little upset about it. And that's when I told her that she'd thank me later. Now I haven't spoken to her since then so I'm wondering if she ever canceled her date with him?" I explained.

"Don't get all worked up. I'm guessing that she went out with him anyway and they're probably laid up in one of those hotel suites on the strip."

"Nah, I know Nancy. She'd never ditch work without calling in sick or something. So, I'm thinking she might've tried to get out of the date but he pressured her to go anyway and did something bad to her."

Dylan chuckled. "Come on Kira, that nigga is a moron but I know he wouldn't hurt a chick because she didn't want to go out with him."

"You can laugh all you want. I know Nancy well enough to know that she wouldn't miss work for no one unless someone was holding her against her will."

Dylan reached towards me and rubbed my arm. "Stop worrying. She's a grown woman so I'm sure she'll show up sometime later today." He said hoping it would make me feel better. Truth be told, I wasn't. There was nothing Dylan could say that would have made me feel any different. I needed proof that Nancy was okay. My gut feeling painted an entirely different story and it wasn't pretty. In other words, time will tell.

Gotta' Watch Your Own Back

People say that what doesn't kill you makes you stronger, but I totally disagree. With everything that I've been through in my lifetime, I felt like I'd died and came back to life. Dealing with street life puts you on an entirely different scale. No matter how much you say you're going to walk away from it, it never happens. The money and the power is addictive. And that will never change.

This is day three and Nancy still hasn't resurfaced so her family has filed a missing persons report on her. I spoke to Nancy's mother on the phone for a brief moment. She asked me questions from when had I last seen Nancy to if I knew who Nancy was dating at the time she went missing? I told her that I didn't have an answer for either of her questions. But if something came up, I would call her. After she accepted the fact that I couldn't help her we ended our call.

I spoke with Jason again as well. He seemed more bent out of shape than I was. There were a few rumors circling around the dealership that they had slept together a few times. There was no way he would take Nancy's disappearance as hard as he had unless he had feelings for her. So I guess those rumors were true.

To get my mind off all the stuff that was going on I decided to go downstairs to the gym area of my apartment building just so I could blow off some steam. Before I could walk out of my apartment my cell phone rang. I stood at the front door and pulled it from my water bottle case. "Hello," I said.

"Hey baby girl, it's your father."

I sucked my teeth because talking to my father was the last thing I wanted to do. "What is it dad?" I asked sarcastically.

"Are you home?" he asked with urgency.

"Yes, I am. Why?"

"Turn the TV channel to Fox One News. There's a reporter at the dealership where you work talking about the receptionist who works there is missing."

A sharp pain shot through my chest. And then a heavy feeling of anxiety struck me next. The truth was about to come out and there was no way that I would be able to avoid it. Instead of brushing my father off, I rushed over to the TV and powered it on. Immediately after I got to a solid picture I sifted through the channels until I got to channel eleven.

Unbelievably I stood there with my mouth slightly ajar while I listened to what the reporter had to say. "Daddy, I'll call you back in a minute." I told him.

I didn't wait for him to say yes. I disconnected the call at that moment.

I took a seat on the sofa in front of the TV and tuned into what the reporter was saying. After sitting there for two and a half minutes I got an earful of information surrounding the disappearance of Nancy. The whole thing was becoming creepier by the minute and Kendrick's boy John's name was all over this. There was no doubt in my mind that John had something to do with Nancy's disappearance. And the only person I shared this with was Dylan. So, instead of calling my father back I called Dylan. Unfortunately for me he didn't answer and I became furious. I needed someone to talk to and Dylan was that person.

Before I could gather my thoughts and decide whether to stay in the house or go downstairs to the gym, the front door opened and Dylan walked in. I let out a sigh of relief. "I just tried to call you." I spoke first.

After he closed the front door and locked it, he walked towards me. "What's up?"

"Remember when I told you that Nancy could be missing?"

"Yeah. Why they found her?"

"No. She's still missing. So, her family filed a missing persons report and they called Fox News so they could run the story."

"How do you know that?"

"Because the news just went off. There was a reporter standing in front of the dealership saying that she was informed that Nancy hadn't been to work in three days and that her family was really worried and if anyone had any information on her whereabouts to please contact the 1-800 number."

"Oh wow! So, I guess you were right."

"You damn right. I knew what I was talking about." I replied in a cocky manner.

"Well, I hope you aren't getting any bright ideas because you know something that Nancy's family doesn't."

"And what does that mean?"

"It means that I don't want you getting involved with it. This is a doggy-dog world we live in and we need to only look out for ourselves."

"Come on Dylan, I am not that stupid."

"Well, that's good to know."

I sucked my teeth and took a seat back down on the sofa. "Why me?" I said aloud.

"Technically it's not you. So, be careful with your words." Dylan replied, his tone was strong and authoritative. I had no other alternative but to listen to him. "Do you know what I want you to do?" he continued.

"No what?"

"That shit that happened to your father's friends and now that chick Nancy has gotten too close to home so today is your last day selling cars." Dylan told me.

"So what am I going to do?" I wanted to know. It didn't bother me that I wasn't going to work at the dealership anymore. What I was concerned about was what I'd be doing during the day? Before all of this drama unfolded, I dreaded being home all day on my days off. So once this thing blows over, I hope I'd be able to go back to a normal life, making my own money. I mean, it's easy to have a man that's a baller, but when you've always had your own money like me, you can't settle for anything outside normalcy.

By the time our conversation ended, Dylan instructed me to lay low while at the apartment until he goes out into the streets to see if anyone is talking about Nancy. "If you want something to eat, call me and I'll bring it to you." He told me.

After I agreed to his instructions he left the apartment. I laid across the living room sofa and pondered on everything that had transpired these last few days. "Please Lord, don't let Nancy be dead." I prayed and laid my head down.

Lying Comes With The Territory

The news station ran footage of Nancy's disappearance every couple of hours. My father called me twice after we spoke the first time, but I elected not to answer his calls. So, he took the liberty by leaving me a voicemail message. *Kira I know you're against me talking to the detective that's heading the Mahoney's murder investigation but I had to reach out to him today after I learned that the young lady name Nancy Cox who is missing, works at the same dealership as you. Coincidentally he says that he remembers talking to her on the day he went up to the dealership to talk to you. And because of that, he wants to speak with you. Please call me back honey. I'm really concerned about your safety. I love you.*

After listening to my father's voicemail message I called him back that instant. "Daddy, I just got your message and I want to know exactly what you told the cop?"

"I can't do that at this moment."

"And why not?"

"Because I'm talking to Detective Grimes."

"Are you down at the police station again?"

"No. Detective Grimes stopped by my house."

"He needs to get out of your house right now daddy."

"I'm sorry darling I can't do that."

"Daddy, you need to listen to me." I said, on the verge of crying. My eyes were being filled up with tears.

"No baby, you need to listen to me. Detective Grimes needs to talk to you about your co-worker Nancy Cox."

"Daddy are you fucking deaf? I told you I am not talking to that man. Now you tell him to leave your house right now!" I screamed through the receiver of my cell phone.

"Kira, this is Detective Grimes and your father and I have you on speaker." I heard the cop say.

"Are you hard of hearing? I told you I didn't have anything to say to you." I yelled.

"Look Kira, I know you're upset and you don't want to talk to me. But I really need your help."

"Why won't y'all leave me alone?" I continued to yell.

"Listen Kira, I have a copy of the surveillance tape from a couple of days ago when you came to work and handed Nancy what looked like an I.D. card."

"And, so what?!" I replied sarcastically.

"Well, not too long after you left, a guy by the name of John Crew stopped by the dealership and was given what looked like the same I.D. card you handed Nancy. Now before John Crew left the dealership, he talked to Ms. Cox for a few minutes and it looked like they were flirting back and forth with one another. So, my question to you is, was that an identification card?"

"I don't remember." I lied.

"Okay, well can you tell me if she ever mentioned to you that she and John saw one another after business hours?"

"Not to my knowledge." I lied once again.

"Are you sure?"

"Yes, I am sure. And now I have to go." I replied and then I disconnected our call.

Once again my father has put me in a compromising situation. And the fact that Detective Grimes wants to tie me to John Crew isn't cool, which is why I lied. I swear I wanted to call him back and tell him to go and fuck himself. Does he not see that I am trying to avoid him at all cost? He can't do a damn thing for me except for get me killed and I won't allow that.

I paced the living room floor at least one hundred times thinking about if Nancy would've listened to me, then she wouldn't be missing and Detective Grimes wouldn't be trying to connect me to John Crew. Why the hell won't people listen when they're given good advise? I told her not to fuck with that nigga but she let her pussy dictate her actions so now she's nowhere to be found. What a way to fuck up your life!

When It Rains It Pours

I thought Dylan would've come back to the apartment by now but until this moment he hasn't. Thankfully my father hasn't tried to reach out to me. But if he had, I wouldn't answer his call. He has become very toxic and I can't tolerate him anymore.

While I was watching TV my cell phone rang. I was happy because I knew it was Dylan. "Hello," I said.

"I got a present for you."

"You got what for me?" I responded nonchalantly. This person on the phone was definitely not Dylan.

"I said I've got a present for you." The voice repeated itself.

Now what I can say is that the voice belongs to a guy, I just can't say who it is. "Who is this?" I asked.

"Don't be so concerned about who I am. What you need to be concerned about is how fast you can get to the alley behind the abandoned warehouse on 53rd Street because that is where you will get your present." The guy continued.

My heart started beating uncontrollably. "Do I have an option?" I asked.

"Fuck no you bitch! You've got an hour to get there. Also make sure you come alone. That means no boyfriend and no cops. Now if you go against our wishes your father will die."

"Oh my God! What do you mean my father? You got my father?" I screamed.

"Shut up! You stupid bitch!"

"Okay, I'm sorry. Please don't hurt my father." I begged.

"Just be at the alley on 53rd in an hour."

"I will be there and I will come alone."

"Good." He said and then the line went dead.

Instead of jumping to my feet and running out of the house to go and save my father, I sat there on the sofa and pondered why was this shit happening to me. I warned my father so many times but yet he let my words roll off his back. How fucking selfish could he be? Dylan warned me about this day. Now, I can't tell him for the fear of my father getting killed. What was I supposed to do?

I finally got up from the sofa but it seemed like I was moving in slow motion. I was literally dreading to leave my apartment without any protection. I knew I couldn't take Dylan or the cops with me so I went into the closet where Dylan kept his jackets and coats and grabbed one of the 9mm glocks he had stashed with his money inside of the safe. I made sure the magazine was filled up and then I made sure the safety was on. I knew I would have to take the safety off before I got to 53rd Street, so that stayed in the forefront of my mind.

Capital Punishment

With only twenty minutes left I raced across town to rescue my father. I had no idea what I was about to walk into but I figured since I had a pistol in hand, the odds could possibly end in my favor.

My heart raced in an uncontrollable speed while anxiety ripped my stomach apart. One part of me wanted to turn around and throw the deuces sign up to my father but the other part of me felt that no matter how stupid or fucked up in the head my father was, I had to save him. He was the only living relative that I had.

When I pulled up to the corner of 53rd Street and 5th Avenue a panic attack hit me at an all time high. My eyes became blurry as I tried to navigate my point of location. "Lord, please let me get out of this alive." I whispered loud enough that only I could hear me.

Suddenly a dark grey van pulled up beside me. I almost jumped out of my fucking skin. The passenger's face was covered with a black ski mask. "Pull up into that warehouse." He yelled.

"Okay," I said, but it was barely audible, waiting for them to go ahead of me.

"Come on let's go. You first." He yelled at me once again.

"Okay. Okay." I said and then I looked down at my lap to make sure I had Dylan's gun within reach and when I realized that I had, I took my foot of the brake and sped off lightly.

The van drove behind me, I'm assuming to make sure I wasn't going anywhere. So, as soon as we both arrived inside of the empty site, I took the safety off and placed the gun in the waist area of my pants and then I pulled my shirt down over it.

"Get out of the car." The passenger yelled. So, I opened the car door and stepped out of the car.

"Let me see your hands." He continued. So, I lifted my hands over my head. Unfortunately for me, Dylan's gun fell to the ground. "She's got a gun!" the driver yelled.

The passenger rushed towards me and knocked me down to the ground. He snatched up the gun quicker than I could blink my eyes. "You trying to shoot me?" he yelled at me, spit shooting from his mouth.

"No. I just brought it for my own protection." I explained.

"Yeah, well try something like that again and you're gonna die." He roared.

"Okay. I'm sorry." I replied in an apologetic way.

"Open up the sliding door." The passenger instructed.

Seconds later the van door slid open and I noticed that there was a guy standing guard in the back of the van holding a handgun just like the one they took from me. In total there were three guys carrying out this operation and I knew that none of them were Kendrick or John Crew.

Sitting in Indian style with blinders covering their eyes and duct tape tied around their mouths and their wrists was my father and Nancy. My heart dropped to the pit of my stomach. I couldn't believe my eyes. Their faces were covered in blood and they both looked like they were beat badly.

By the looks of Nancy's clothes I could tell that they kidnapped her the same day I told her to cancel her date with John. They must've gotten my father today. "Oh my God! What are you going to do with them?" I asked. I wanted so badly to hear them say that they were going to let them both go.

"We're going to let him go. But she's staying with us because she ratted you out. She told us everything you told her." The passenger said.

Nancy heard her fate and started screaming and crying. "No! Please let me go! I promise I won't say anything." She pleaded with him.

"Sorry, but your time is up." He said and then he looked at the person who opened up the sliding door and motioned for him to shoot Nancy and that's what he did. POW! It only took one shot and Nancy's brain splattered all over the back of the van while her body collapsed onto the floor.

I swear I couldn't believe my eyes. It felt like a bad dream. But when I blinked my eyes, I realized that this shit was real. These guys aren't playing any fucking games. They killed Nancy without hesitation so I knew that my father and I could easily end up just like Nancy.

"Make this your final warning." The passenger said and then he turned his focus back on the guy that shot and killed Nancy. "Get rid of him." He instructed.

Seconds later, the guy pushed my father out of the van and onto the ground. The guy who did all the talking got back into the van and then the van sped off. I ran over to my father, snatched the blindfold from his eyes and kissed him over a dozen times while the tears from my eyes coated the skin on my face. "Daddy, I love you. I'm so glad you're still alive." I told him.

I held him for the next couple of minutes without letting him go. All I could think about was how quickly Nancy's life was taken from her. The thought of her body lying on the floor of that van put a new fear in my heart. And now I need to figure out how to get my father not to tell the cops what happened. If he doesn't come on board with me then he will definitely end up like Nancy.

STAY TUNED

Wifey's

NEXT DEADLY HUSTLE

AVAILABLE NOW

Sneak Peek into the
"Green Eye Bandit"
(E-book & Paperback Available Now)

Green Eye Bandit

PROLOGUE

My heart wouldn't accept what was going on around me. But my eyes knew better. Watching these monsters torture my sister Shelby had become unbearable. And every time I tried to look away, one of those goons snatched my head back by yanking my hair. "Nah bitch, you're gonna watch this." The guy roared and then he spit in my face.

My sister Shelby and I had always played a game or two of Russian roulette with our lives, but as fate would have it, our time had ran out. There was no way we were going to walk out of here alive. Even

Shelby's probation officer Ms. Welch wasn't going to leave out of here breathing. Unfortunately, for her she planned an after hours home visit to our apartment so she could check on Shelby, and walked into a death trap. I knew she wished she had kept her field visits during business hours because now she's gotten herself into a bloody mess.

There were three guys surrounding us. They kicked in our front door and bum rushed our apartment with their guns drawn and ready to fire. I knew why they were here so I tried to escape out of the apartment from our second story bathroom window, but Rocko quickly apprehended me and started the beating.

All three men looked menacing. They were average in height but they made up for their height in weight. They had to be at least two hundred pounds easy because the first time Shelby and I got hit in the face, it sounded like our jawbones cracked. Shelby screamed from the minute Rocko snatched her up by her neck until the time he hit her in her face. I saw the horror in her eyes and I saw our lives flash right before my eyes. It was going to be a sad night for the both of us. God help us all.

Breon and his henchmen came equipped with rope and duct tape, and tied us up to our kitchen chairs so we wouldn't have another chance to run. They even tied gags around our mouths to prevent us from letting the outside world know what was going on inside of our apartment. And it worked, because half way into the beating, Ms. Welch knocked on the front door. "Open the door Ms. Martin, it's me Ms. Welch." We all heard her say.

All three men looked at one another and then they looked at Shelby and I. The guy Breon wanted to know who was at the door. He pulled the duct tape from Shelby's mouth good enough for her to answer his questions. "It's my P.O. and she isn't going to leave until somebody opens the door," she warned him.

Breon motioned one of the guys to look through the peephole to see what Shelby's probation officer was doing on the other side of the door. The guy tiptoed to the front door and when he stepped on the loose wooden board directly in front of the door, it cracked and Ms. Welch heard it loud and clear. "Shelby, I hear you in there. Now if you don't open this door right now, I am going to have the police come and do it for me," she threatened, but no one moved. Breon waited for a moment to think and then a couple seconds later he instructed the guy at the door to open the door. "What if she wants to come in?" he objected.

"Just shut up and open it." Breon demanded in a low like whisper. But his pitch wasn't low enough because Ms. Welch heard him. "I hear you all talking in there. Now this will be the last time I tell you to open this door before I call the police for their assistance," she warned us.

The guy at the front door looked back at Breon once more. "Do it now." Breon instructed him once again. I could see that Breon was getting a little aggravated. The guy saw it too and decided to do as he was told. He turned back towards the front door and pulled the mask from his head. And not even a second later, he unlocked and opened the front door. The way our chairs were placed around the kitchen table, Shelby couldn't see the front door but I could.

Ms. Welch stood there before him and went into question mode that instant. "Where is Shelby?" she asked him.

"She's not here," the guy lied.

Ms. Welch sensed that he lied too, that's why she tried to look around him to get a good look into the apartment. The guy was too quick for her and moved to block her view. She didn't like that one bit. "Are you trying to hide something from me?" she questioned him once more.

"No, I'm not."

"What is your name young man?" her questions continued.

"My name is Antonio." He said flatly.

"Well Mr. Antonio, my name is Ms. Welch and I am Shelby's probation officer. And I am here today because she lied to me about sending in copies of her check stubs. Now, I'm going to need you to step aside so I can enter into this apartment."

"But I told you she's not here."

"I remember you saying that, but as her probation officer I have the right to search her dwelling at which time I see fit. And today would be one of those times," she tried to say it as politely as she could. Ms. Welch was one evil ass lady and when it came to home visits, she meant business. And the fact that this guy wasn't going to allow her to do what she wanted, she wasn't too happy about that.

While all of the commotion went on at the front door, Breon realized that his sidekick wasn't handling the situation with Shelby's probation officer as swiftly as he'd liked, so he stormed to the front door with his gun behind his back to see if he could make her go away. But what Breon failed to do was cover Shelby's mouth up before he walked off and left us in the kitchen. And as soon as Breon turned the corner, Shelby screamed as loud as she could and said, "Ms. Welch run and call the police."

Breon turned back around and rushed towards Shelby. When he got within arms reach of her, he lunged back and punched her in the face as hard as he could. The force behind his punch knocked Shelby backwards onto the floor. And when I thought I'd seen enough, he started kicking her in her side while her arms were tied behind her back and her ankles tied to the legs of the chair. She looked so helpless on the floor and I couldn't do a thing to help her. She cried her poor heart out while Breon kicked and stomped her with his fucking Timberland boots. I swear if I had the strength to break loose from these restraints, I'd have his fucking head on a chopping block, digging his eyes out of his fucking head.

While Breon was beating the shit out of my sister, the other guy had no choice but to grab Ms. Welch and drag her into the apartment. She put up a big fight to get away from him but when Breon's other henchman saw that his partner needed help in getting Ms. Welch under control, he went to his aid. With both men attacking her at the same time, Ms. Welch didn't have a fighting chance. And after she suffered consistent blows to her body and head, she lost consciousness.

"Breon, we gon' need some help picking her big ass up from the floor. I heard one guy say.

"One of y'all help me pick this bitch up from the floor first." Breon demanded. He had stopped hitting and kicking Shelby by this time. So, after Breon and one of the other guys helped sit Shelby's chair back on it's feet, all three of them managed to pick Ms. Welch up and sat her in a chair next to us. They didn't waste any time bounding and gagging her.

I could tell that she was clinging onto life. And right before the beating started, she begged those fucking monsters to spare her. "I'm not the one you want." She pleaded. But they ignored her cries and proceeded to beat her across her face. I literally cried for her and Shelby, because I felt their pain and I knew that my time was coming next.

Breon's heartless ass washed Shelby's blood from his arms and hands. He dried them off by wiping his palms directly across the thigh part of his jeans. I watched him very closely through my glassy eyes. I was furious about everything I had witnessed and I wanted my revenge. But that feat looked impossible from where I was sitting, so I sat quickly and prayed a silent prayer.

"Don't close those green eyes now bitch! 'Cause your ass is next." Breon warned me and then I heard his footsteps coming in my direction. I stopped midway in my prayer and opened my eyes. I tried to scream when I saw that he had his gun pointed directly at Shelby, but I was unable to do so with the duct tape wrapped tightly around my mouth. Tears started falling rapidly. And my heart began to beat erratically. She was done and I knew it. So, I took one last look at her and watched Breon pull the trigger. BOOM!

Green Eye Bandit

<u>Chapter One – The Come Up</u>

The temperature throughout the hotel suite was set at 70 degrees, but sweat pellets emerged from the pores of my forehead and underneath my armpits like I was sitting inside of a fucking sauna. I swear I couldn't get out of this place quick enough. I had just taken a bunch of cash from a black, Marc Jacobs handcrafted leather wallet that belonged to this guy my sister Shelby was fucking in the next room. When I first arrived in the hotel room, I heard Shelby moaning like her mind was going bad. It sounded like she was getting her pussy ate and when I peeped in on the action, my suspicions were confirmed. That cracker she had feasting between her legs was putting in overtime. I almost got up the nerve to ask him to give me some of his tongue action. But after I snapped back into reality about what I came there to do, I decided against it.

A few minutes after I started going through the man's things, I realized he and Shelby had switched positions. "Damn girl, you sure know how to suck the meat off my dick!" I heard him say to Shelby.

"I make you……..feel……..good, huh?" Shelby replied between licks.

I laughed of course because Shelby was a class act. She was a master at making guys weak at their knees. Shelby was a sexy, 135lbs., bombshell. She was a very pretty young woman with a body to die for. Her caramel complexion, long, straight, dark brown hair, and her big hazel colored eyes were the perfect combination. It wasn't hard to tell that she was half Cuban and black. From the time we were young girls, boys would always throw themselves at her. And while she had them literally eating out of her hands, she could never keep a man around long enough to have a solid relationship, so she did the next best thing; trick with them. She gave them what they wanted and in return they gave her what she wanted. It was a win-win situation in her eyes.

The joker she had in her grasp tonight was a white investment banker from Maryland in town for a conference. According to the driver's license in his wallet, his name was Alex Leman. He was born in 1962, he resided in the city of Baltimore, and he was an organ donor. How freaking patriotic of him? The old dude had a soft spot for humanity. Sorry to say he had a kinky side to him as well. And since tonight was his last night in town, Shelby and I seized this opportunity to come up on some major dough. I got him for every crisp one hundred dollar bill he had tucked away in his wallet. I hadn't had a chance to count them, but there had to be at least twelve of them in all. He also had a few major credit cards like an American Express and Discover card, but I left them alone. I wasn't about to get caught on camera in some department store trying to buy a bunch of bullshit with stolen credit cards. I wanted my money free and clear. Too bad, I can't say the same about Shelby. She'd snatch this guy's credit cards up in a heartbeat. It didn't matter to her that she was on probation, because she had already been charged and convicted of credit card fraud a year ago. But I cared and as long as she turned the tricks and I did the taking, I vowed to do things my way.

Immediately after I had taken all of the money this guy Alex had, I stuffed it inside of my pants pocket and headed towards the door of the hotel suite. But before I could sneak back out of the hotel room, some asshole knocked on the fucking door. I panicked and almost pissed in my pants. How in the hell could someone come at a time like this? I rushed to the door and looked through the peephole. To my surprise, my co-worker Mitch from room service was standing on the other side of the door with a bottle of champagne in a bucket of ice and two champagne glasses placed on a rolling table. My first reaction was to open the door and tell Mitch to carry his ass, but then I realized how he'd react seeing me in this room, so I decided against it. Two seconds later, Mitch knocked on the door again and then he yelled out the words, "Room service."

I literally almost passed out right there in the hallway. But when I heard Alex scramble to his feet to get the door, I jumped into the hallway closet and slid the door closed. "I'm coming," I heard Shelby's sex partner yell as soon as he got within several feet of the door to his suite.

I couldn't see Alex as he made his way to the door, but I heard every move he made from the time he opened the door to let Mitch roll the table inside the room until he started questioning Shelby, who had followed him to the door. "Wait a minute," he said and then he fell silent.

"What's the matter?" Shelby questioned him.

"I had over fifteen hundred dollars in my fucking wallet and now it's gone." he said.

"Are you sure?" Shelby asked.

"You goddamn right I'm sure!" he roared.

"Why are you snapping at me?" I heard Shelby say.

"Because my money is gone and you've been the only one in this room."

"So, you're accusing me of taking your fucking money? she snapped back.

"Who else could've taken it?" Alex stood his ground.

"First of all, I've been by your side the entire time I've been in this fucking room. So, how in the hell could I have taken the money?" Shelby reasoned.

Before Alex responded to Shelby, Mitch interjected, "Sir, don't worry about it. Just call room service and have them charge the champagne and the strawberries to your room." Then I heard the door close.

Seconds later, I heard Shelby say, "I can't believe you just accused me of stealing your fucking money."

But Alex didn't respond to her. He remained completely quiet. They continued to stand outside of the closet door, so I was literally in the center of all the action. I just wished that I could see what they were doing.

"Why the fuck are you just standing there and looking at me like you're insane?" Shelby continued.

So again, I waited to hear Alex's response. And to my surprise, he didn't utter one word. I did however hear sudden movement and then I heard a loud boom sound. "What the fuck are you doing? Get off of me." Shelby said, her voice was barely audible.

"I going to kill you, you black bitch!" he grinded his teeth. "You're gonna wish you never laid eyes on me." He continued.

Then I heard Shelby coughing. "Get off me!" She managed to say.

My heart raced as I listened to the commotion outside of the closet door. It was apparent that Alex was choking Shelby to her death. And that's when it popped in my head that if I didn't stop him, I'd have one dead sister. So, within seconds, I burst out of the closet door and was able to witness first hand how badly Alex was hurting her.

Right after I burst onto the scene, I noticed how shocked they both were to see me. "Get the fuck off of her!" I demanded as I stormed towards his 5'10 frame. He looked like he weighed 150lbs., but that didn't at all intimidate me, even though I was at least 30lbs., lighter. I used to run track back when I was in high school, so I was physically fit.

"What the fuck?" Alex uttered from his lips. He was definitely at a lost for words when he realized that he and Shelby weren't alone. And while he had Shelby's back against the wall, he had both of his hands around her neck, leaving himself vulnerable for me to intervene. This guy was on a mission to choke the life out of her. So I lunged towards the back of his head with my fist and clocked him as hard as I could. I followed that blow with several more punches, and then I threw my right arm around his neck and grabbed him into a chokehold. "Let her go." I demanded as I applied pressure to his neck.

He struggled to keep Shelby within his grasp and when he realized that I wasn't going to let him go, he started loosening the grip around her neck and then he finally let her go. "Alright. I let her go. Now you let me go," he pleaded.

"If I let you go, you ain't gonna try no funny shit, right?" I questioned him.

"No. I swear I won't." he assured me. But I wasn't feeling his answer. Something told me that this guy couldn't be trusted. He had already tried to murk Shelby, so why wouldn't he try to throw shade on both of us in this damn hotel room? If he really wanted to fuck us over, he could call the cops on our asses and get me and Shelby locked up for trespassing and robbery and that would not have been a good look on our part.

"How do I know if you'll try some dumb shit?" I asked him.

"Look, lady I don't want any problems. Just take your friend and leave and I'll forget that any of this happened." He managed to say while I continued to hold him in the chokehold.

I looked at Shelby who was only three feet away from me. I searched her face for any sign about which course of action we should take. And when she instructed me to keep him hemmed up until she gathered up her things, I did just that. "A'ight. But hurry up." I yelled aloud as she disappeared into the other room.

Meanwhile Alex became a little antsy while I had him in the chokehold. "You do know that I could have both of you bitches arrested" he commented.

I tightened the grip around his neck just a bit more. "Shut the hell up before I call your wife and tell her how you like eating black pussy." I said.

After I threatened to spill the beans on his ass, he immediately changed his tune. "Look, just get out of my hotel room and take your friend with you," he said.

Moments later, Shelby showed back up fully dressed with her handbag clutched tightly in her right hand. "Come on, let's go." she said. And then she rushed towards the door. ....,

Once Shelby had the door opened, I released my grip from the white guy's neck and raced out of the door behind her. She and I ran into the hallway and bumped into Mitch. Mitch was a middle aged, metrosexual white guy with feminine behavior and everything to prove. He stood there with mere shock written all over his face. But I was even more shocked than anything. I thought he'd carried his ass back to the kitchen, but I was so wrong. And now that Shelby and I were caught red handed, I needed to come up with something really quick. Mitch was one of the hotel's ass kissers. He'd blow the whistle on anyone if it meant he'd get a promotion. So, I knew whatever I said to him had to be convincing or else. "Mitch, what's going on?" I asked trying to prevent myself from panting. I had just ran out of a man's hotel room after holding him against his will, so I was very tired.

"Well, I was on my way back to room 521 to make sure everything was okay with our guest and his female companion." Mitch began to say and then he turned his attention towards Shelby. "And from the looks of it, I can see that she's fine."

I knew Mitch was being a smart ass. And I played along. "Yeah, she's fine. Luckily, I was still at work when she called me to come and talk some sense into that guy. And thank God he managed to find his money just as we were about to leave." I lied.

"Lucky her." he replied sarcastically.

"Well, I appreciate the fact that you thought about her enough to come all the way back up here to check on her. That's noble of you." I replied with a fake smile.

"I was actually more concerned about Mr. Leman," he pointed out.

"Well, it doesn't matter. Either way your intentions were good, so keep up the good work." I told him and then I gave him a pat on the shoulder and made my way to the stairwell. Shelby followed down behind me like she was my shadow. I figured it was best to leave the hotel by taking the stairs just in case that white cat Alex had a change of heart and wanted to call security on our asses. Besides that, I didn't want to run into another one of my co-workers. Seeing Mitch was enough for one night.

Thankfully, Shelby and I made it out the hotel without running into another one of my co-workers, plus we were fifteen hundred dollars richer. On our way up Atlantic Avenue, she and I both laughed at how stupid that white guy looked after he realized that his money had been taken. I even elaborated about how he looked when he saw me jump out of the closet. "Did you see the look on his face after he realized I was in the room with y'all?" I said.

"Yeah, I saw it. But check it out; I was even more shocked to see you myself. I thought you had already left the room when the room service guy came."

"Did you even know that he ordered room service?" I asked while she drove us away from the hotel.

"No. I didn't. I'm thinking he probably did it before I got to his room."

"Yeah, he probably did." I agreed with Shelby while I divided up the proceeds from tonight's mission. Right after I handed Shelby her cut of the money, I stuffed the other portion down into my handbag. She held it up in the air and said, "There's nothing like fucking a dude for some cold hard cash."

I smiled. "And I'm sure you mean that in the most sincerest fashion."

"Why of course." She smiled back. "Too bad, we don't have another dummy lined up for tonight."

"Stop being greedy. One sucker per night is enough. And besides, after that shit that went down tonight, you should be ready to go home and chill." I said.

Shelby laughed at me like I had just made a joke. "You are so fucking paranoid. That guy was just as scared as we were. You heard him when he told us to get out of his room. He wanted us to leave more than we did."

"Yeah, but what if we were dealing with a different guy? Some random asshole that didn't have shit to lose." I pointed out.

"Stop being so dramatic." Shelby said with intentions to downplay the situation.

"How am I being dramatic? You and I rob niggas on a daily basis. And so far we've been on easy street. But, who's to say that our luck isn't going to run out?"

"Tina please don't beat me in the head. We got what we went there for and now we're on our way home. So, chill out will ya'?"

"I 'ma chill out. But so you know, we can't let what happened tonight ever happen again. Agreed?"

Shelby let out a long sigh and then she said, "Yeah. Agreed."